Shorty Fell in Love With a Dope Boy 2
By: A. Jova'n

Synopsis:

Rerelease

"You don't know what you have until it's gone." That statement rang true for Church, when it came to how he felt about Kiarra. Acting on impulse, Church snatched Kiarra, not thinking about the consequences of his actions. With a pregnant girlfriend at home, Church have a last minute change of heart. But, is it too late with Kiarra's very dangerous God father Law back in town?

Kiarra finds herself in a situation that she's not sure she can get out of alive. Fearing for her safety, as well as the safety of the baby, Kiarra need to think of a way to get out untouched. After she's saved by an unsuspected friend by the name of Kodi, she find herself trying to return the favor.

Since Kiarra's disappearance, Deontae was ready to turn in his scalpel for a pistol, in order to get his girl back. When she's returned safely, it gives the couple a chance to focus on the excitement of bringing their little person into the world.

Lauren was unlucky with love when it came to her relationship with Tre. But, when she met up and coming rapper Banks, he opened her eyes to what it's like to be with a real man. But when they're faced with his stalker ex girlfriend, does Banks proves that he was too good to be true, or can Banks fight temptation to keep him and Lauren's relationship afloat?

To bring awareness to Domestic Violence, I'm introducing to another person who fell victim to loving a dope boy. Meet Kodi Anderson, she's been with her boyfriend Gates for 6 years, and it's been everything but a fairytale. Gates have a drinking, cheating, and a problem keeping his hands to himself. When Gates moved them to Chicago, so he could pick up work with Church and Tre, he made a promise to change his ways. Can he keep that promise, or will Kodi's love story end in tragedy?

We all want that perfect love story, but that's impossible when Shorty Fell in Love with a Dope Boy Too.

Contact Me:

Facebook: A Jova'n

Instagram: a.jovan__

Follow my Facebook group 'A. Jova'n's Reading Haven for sneak peeks and discussion!

Where we left off...

July 2000

"Kiarra! Chubbz, come downstairs please!"

Hearing my daddy yell my name had me jumping up from the floor and sprinting downstairs. When I finally found him in the living room, I smiled and jumped into his arms.

"Hi Daddy, I missed you reading my story last night, you know Mommy can't do the voices like you. Can you stay home and play operation with me?"

I didn't know exactly what my dad did for work, but he was gone a lot and sometimes, he went on trips without me and Mommy. He always brought me something back, so that kept my 10-year-old self happy.

"Whatever you want, baby girl, but you know what we have to do today."

Every Saturday, my dad would wake me up and we would meet up with Lauren and Uncle Law for 'survival training'. We were ten; what kind of survival did we need? I don't know, but for the past two years, it had been our routine, so I was already dressed and ready to go.

Running upstairs, I gave my mom a kiss and met my dad back at the door.

"Ok, I'm ready, Daddy."

Walking out to my father's 2000 Mercedes Benz E Class, I smiled as he opened the back door for me. Once I got in, I secured my seat belt and sat back.

"Ki, you make sure when you you're old enough to date, they always treat you like the princess you are. They better open and hold doors or they're going to have to deal with your old man, you hear me?"

"Yes Daddy, but why can't I ride in the front with you?" I folded my arms across my chest and stared at him while he reversed out of the driveway. I hated always being in the back I felt like a baby.

"Because, you're safer in the back, I can protect you." That didn't make sense because I was all the way back here. Instead of saying anything else, I just stared out the window and waited until we got to our destination.

Thirty minutes later, when we pulled into a wooded area and parked. I waited for my dad to open my door before I got out. When my feet touched the ground, my dad gave me a hug and kissed me on the forehead.

"Don't be mad at daddy, Ki. Everything I do is to make sure you're always taken care of." Staring into my daddy's hazel eyes that mirrored mine, I just said okay and laid my head on his chest.

A black Yukon Denali pulled up a few feet away from us, and my body stiffened a little. Sensing my nervousness, my dad rubbed my back, telling me to relax. When I saw Uncle Law get out and walk around to the passenger back door, I pushed my dad away and ran to the truck.

"Lauren!" I was happy to see my best friend. Since they

moved from next door to us, I don't see her as much.

"Dang, just push your old man down," my dad joked, walking up and giving Uncle Law dap.

"Sorry daddy!"

"Look Ki, my daddy bought me a new camera." Lauren showed me the camera she had in the backseat with her; she loved taking pictures. Sometimes when I stayed at her house, she would want to play dress up and take pictures of me in different clothes.

"Come on girls, let's go," Uncle Law called out, and we followed behind them through the woods.

"Lauren, ask my dad can you come over. I'll get some old clothes from my mom to model for you." I knew he would tell me to ask my mom first, but if Lauren asked, he'd say yes to her.

"Ok yaaay! I can't wait."

We walked about 10 minutes until we were walking

up to a cabin with all type of big guns laid out on the porch. Usually when they had us shooting, it was small guns. I don't know what this was about. Judging by the confused look on Lauren's face, she didn't know either.

"So, first thing I wanted to go over with you girls is what to do if you're ever in a dangerous situation and you're alone. If you have a phone, you will text one of three people, each other, your mother, or your father. All you'll have to send is 'family.' Once we get that message, we'll know it's an emergency and will be able to find and help you as soon as possible. Do you two got that?" Uncle Lawrence spoke up when we reached the porch.

"Yes, sir," we spoke up at the same time.

"Good, don't ever forget that."

"Princess, you need to wake up and fight."

Suddenly, my dad and everyone else started to fade.

"Ki baby, where are you? I'm so worried."

I was hearing Lauren's voice, but I didn't see her. "Lauren, where are you?"

"God, please let her be ok." I saw Lauren kneeled down praying, but when I tried to touch her, my hand went through her arm. I started panicking and running down a long hall. I needed to find a way out of whatever this was.

My ears started ringing and I dropped down to my knees, covering them up.

"I told you I wasn't letting you leave me, bitch."

My eyes popped open and I was in the back of a car. I was able to peek up and saw the back of Church's head. My eyes were heavy and I was trying so hard not to give in. Peeking out the window, I saw all the expressway signs passing. He was going too fast, so I couldn't read what they said.

My hand went to my pocket before I remembered that he smashed my phone. The pain in my head was returning, and I had no choice but to close my eyes.

"He'll never have you, Kiarra, you're mine. I told you, I fucking told you," was the last thing I heard before everything went black.

ONE

Church

*"I know a way a nigga living is whack but you don't get
a nigga back like that
You got me smoking this black, thinking, sipping this yak
Mind racing now I'm mad, now I'm gripping this gat"*
-Young M.A.

I was sitting back listening to Young M.A 'Karma Krys', and it was like this shit described my feelings perfectly. I had been watching Kiarra for a while, and when saw her with somebody else looking happy, I was ready to lose it all.

"How many times are you gone play this song, it's old as hell Church." Miranda came in the living room and turned the radio down.

"Imma play this shit until I'm done listening to it. If you don't wanna hear it, get out."

"You really gone kick me and your daughter out, while I'm pregnant with your son?"

"I said YOU can get the fuck out, not my daughter. Matter fact, I'm out, I'll be back." I grabbed my black Chicago Bulls hat, and left out the door.

I rode down Lake Shore Drive, smoking my blunt with no destination in mind. Ki was still on my mind heavy and I wanted to go talk to her. I pulled up to her building, and I didn't see her car anywhere, so I was gone sit outside and wait for her ass, but I know if she seen my car she was gone flip the fuck out.

"Yo?"

"I'm bout to send you an address, I need a throw away, asap."

"Got you boss."

I waited for the new car and scrolled through Kiarra's Facebook and Instagram pages. She had been posting more, that's how I was able to keep up with her most of the time. I saw a rusted Ford Taurus pull up, and one of my runners got out to hand me the keys.

"Park my shit at my crib, don't go nowhere else, don't scratch my shit, and don't touch shit or that's yo ass."

"What you got going on, you need me to stay and be look out?"

"What the fuck did I tell you to do? Did I tell yo simple ass to stand the fuck out here to bring attention to me?"

He held his hand up in surrender, and stepped back. "My fault, I was just checking." He got in my car, and I pulled the Taurus around to the back of the building.

I walked into Ki's building and waited until she showed up. I don't even know if she was going to coming back to her place, but it was worth a try.

I was sitting in an uncomfortable ass corner when I finally heard the elevator ding, and then Kiarra's voice.

"I hope I have a boy, I think it'll be fun."

"Oh, so you about to have that nigga's baby huh?" I pulled my gun out and had it pressed against her back. I was itching to pull the trigger, but I don't think I could do it.

I saw her doing something on her phone so I took it and threw it against the wall. "Get the fuck back on the elevator." She did as I said, and we rode the elevator down to the main floor, and we walked out to the back to the waiting car. The thing about being with somebody for a long time, you know them like the back of your hand.

"Baby, I know you better than that, please don't make me do you dirty like this. That's my last warning."

Pow!

She tried to reach for her gun in her purse again so I hit her with my gun, and it accidently went off.

"Fuck! Get the fuck up and get in the back!" Ki was on the ground holding her stomach, so I snatched her up by the hair and was about to throw her in the backseat.

"Please just let me go Church, I'm pregnant, don't do anything stupid!"

Wham!

I sent a blow to her face that made her body go limp, and I had to catch her before she hit the ground again. I threw across the seat and sped off away from the building. I'm sure someone heard the gunshot and was going to be calling the police soon. I didn't plan on shit going left like that but it's too late to turn back now.

"Why you couldn't just work it out with me Ki?

Look what you made me do baby, this aint what I wanted for us. He'll never have you, Kiarra, you're mine, you'll always be mine. I told you, I fucking told you." I was talking aloud, but I knew Kiarra couldn't answer me, she could hear me though.

I pulled up to my house in Indiana and parked in the garage. No one, except Tre knew where it was, but he aint have a reason to come here. I carried Ki in the house and laid her across the bed I had in the basement. She was still knocked out so I just left her down there and went to grab a bottle of Corona out the fridge.

Tre was blowing me up and I sent him to voice-mail. I needed to figure out what I was going to do, so whatever he wanted, he had to take care of it himself.

TWO

Tre

"Did he answer?"

"Do you see me talking on the phone?"

Lauren popped up at my house telling me I needed to call Church because Kiarra was still missing, but I can't see my bro snatching no bitch up, no offense to Ki.

"Don't get fucking smart Tristan, I'm trying to find my best friend that yo retarded ass brother pulled up on. I swear if he hurt her imma kill him myself."

"Aint nobody killing shit, I don't give a fuck what he did, that's my brother and I'll paint this city red if something happened to him."

"Is that a threat?"

"Call it whatever the fuck you want, you can deliver that message to yo nigga too."

"Naw, it aint my nigga you gotta worry about clown."

"Man, gone you heard what I said, I got a team just like the next nigga."

She grabbed her purse and walked to the door. "Well I hope you got them on standby fuck boy."

I didn't know what the fuck been going on with Church ass but he been slacking on his duties lately, and that shit is bad for business. A few times, I had some niggas calling me saying they ran out of product and Church wasn't answering. Now I'm hearing he dun snatched Ki up while he got his pregnant girl and daughter back at home... the nigga clearly lost his shit.

I knew I had to find him before anybody else did, especially if Lo called her pops already. A war isn't something I'm tryna be in the middle of right now, but if it came down to it then... it is what it is, I'm riding with my brother.

I grabbed my keys and went to Church and Miranda's house. I saw all his cars parked out front, so maybe this nigga was home after all.

I ran up the few steps leading to the front door, and banged on the door.

Boom! Boom! Boom!

Miranda opened the door with her huge belly poking out, and a scowl etched on her face. "Yo where Church at?"

"I don't know, he ran outta here yesterday and never came back, now he not answering the damn phone."

"Damn aite." I turned to walk away and I heard Miranda smack her lips before she slammed the front door. It was something about Miranda that just rubbed me the wrong way, the bitch was sneaky, but Church was a grown ass man and I aint getting in his shit. I drove around checking a few of our stash houses looking for Church, and I still didn't see him anywhere.

I pulled into Kenwood liquors on 63rd street to grab me some Swishers, and a bottle of Remy. When I was walking back to my car a blacked out Suburban came whipping in parking lot and almost hit me.

"What the fuck?" The driver's door opened, and I saw this nigga Banks get out like he was standing on something. He walked up to me and I stuffed my hands in my pocket, I wasn't worried about this nigga doing shit to me.

"Where yo brother at?"

"In his skin nigga, fuck you asking for?"

"You lucky I gotta go home to my girl or I'll peel yo shit out here boy."

"Nigga you mean my girl? I'm just letting you borrow her… shit she was just at my crib earlier. Ask her how I took care of that for her." He reached behind him and I still stood in with my hands in my pocket, not moved at all. I aint scared of death, I'll welcome the shit with open arms if it's my time.

"Yo, G come on that aint what we came out here for." A tall ass dark skin nigga with a deep ass Barry White voice, got out the passenger side and pulled Banks back.

"I'll see you around fuck boy."

"Yeah nigga you will, keep playing with my girl, and you gone share a plot with yo brother."

"Ask Lo what I had to say about that." I got in my car and pulled off to go to Sam's house. This nigga had me hot talking that big shit, Lo better get her nigga before I let my gun talk for me next time.

The difference between me and that clown was he rapped about the shit while I do this for real.

Church called me back when I pulled in front of Sam's house, so I put the car in park, and answered the phone.

"Where the fuck you been at nigga, I called yo ass like 10 times?"

"I'm chilling wassup?"

"Nigga, why the fuck did Lo bring her lil' ass to my crib talking about you did something to Kiarra?"

"Her ass aint got it all, so I can't answer that question for you."

"Bro, I don't know what the fuck you got going on, but you need to get yo shit together. I got niggas calling me talking about you MIA when it's money involved, now you over here on some *Taken* shit snatching women."

"I gotta go, I aint snatch shit."

He hung, and I turned my car off, and walked into Sam's house. I know that on one for real now.

THREE

Banks

"Come on G, you can't be catching bodies like that, especially with all them witnesses outside. You got too much to lose to be acting reckless out here."

Deontae call himself preaching to me, like he wasn't talking murdering Church last night.

"Yeah I hear yo bro." I sped to my house, and for Lauren's sake her ass better be there.

If she was still entertaining this nigga, after she call herself in a relationship with me, I was about to turn up on her ass for real.

I walked in the house with Deontae trailing behind me, and I saw Lauren coming down the stairs, wearing a tight ass jogging suit.

"Where you going dressed like that?" She looked up from her phone, and raised her eyebrow.

"Dressed like what Giovanni?"

"That shit tight as hell, is that what you wore to that nigga's house? Yeah, I know about that shit, fuck you being sneaky for?"

"First of all, I don't care if you know about it or not, it wasn't a fucking secret. I went to get him to call his brother, then I left. Now, I'm going to meet my mama and daddy, if yo attitude aint in check I will not be back." She pushed me and switched her big booty ass out the door.

"She be checking yo ass." Deontae said laughing and sitting on the couch.

"Nigga fuck you." His phone rang and he ignored whoever it was and put the phone back in his pocket.

"I keep getting paged, but I can't go in there with Kiarra on my mind like this."

"Sis good, I got some niggas looking out for Church, I'll follow yo lead on where you wanna go with it after that."

"I just want my girl found safely, I aint tryna be the reason another black man is murdered."

"Fuck that shit, yo ass became a doctor and got soft. I'll take a nigga's whole family out if he fucks with mine. I can't go a gun point bro."

"I aint gone lie, the shit I said sound good, and the longer she's missing, the more my mind is changing."

"Well, if you want nigga to keep his life, I'll try my best. You just go figure out what you gone do about the hospital, let them niggas know you taking some emergency leave or some shit."

"Aite bro." he dapped me up and walked out to his truck. I sat down on the couch and texted Lauren. We both got these explosive personalities so we bumped heads a lot, but when we were good, shit was great.

When you gone be back ma?

Idk

Stop playing I'm sorry

Ok, I'll text you when I leave from with my parents

I closed out of our text thread, and responded back to some emails I had waiting. I needed to get to the studio finish this album off, but I can't focus that until I help Tae get his girl back. My burner phone rang and I answered it quick.

"Yo?"

"I got the word out that it's a price on Church, how we taking him?"

"For now, leave his heart beating."

"Heard you."

I disconnected the call, and got my note pad to work on some songs to some beats I was sent.

*****

Lauren walked in the house a few hours later looking like she had been crying. "Come here Lo."

"Banks, I swear if you about to start some shit with me."

"Damn baby, I'm Banks now? What's wrong, you been crying and shit?"

"I'm just worried about Ki, I know y'all got it covered, but I feel like it's something more I need to be doing."

"You damn sure bet not be at that nigga Tre house no mo."

"Okaaayyy, it's not even that serious."

"Right let me go to one of my old hoes cribs, let's see if it's that serious." Her head snapped up at me and I saw her left eye twitch.

"Yeah, you see where yo mind went? My shit went there too. Now you see how I feel."

"Ok, I'm sorry, I wasn't thinking, you mad at me bae?"

"Get yo crazy ass off me man, you was ready to kill my ass two seconds ago, now you wanna get all sweet and shit."

"Whatever, don't say I aint try. Where did Deontae go?"

"I think he went to tell the hospital he wasn't gone be in. What yo people was talking about?"

"Nothing really just checking on me. My mama asked where you was at though, they might stop by to-morrow."

"Awww shit—"

"Don't be extra."

"Don't be hating when yo moms love me more than you."

"I'm not worried about it."

She laid down so her feet was in my lap, and she turned on one of them dumb ass reality shows she always watching. I wouldn't dare be on no Love and Hip hop, shit be fake as fuck.

I put my *Beats* on, and drowned out the world around me while I wrote. I needed to get to s studio asap, but I wasn't gone focus on that until after this shit with Church is taken care of.

FOUR

Kiarra

My eyes opened and I was in a dark room that didn't belong to me. I tried to sit up but the pain in my head had me laying right back down. Memories of what happened started coming back, and I felt the lump on my head. I heard footsteps over my head and I start looking around for anything I could use as a weapon. Church appeared at the bottom of the stairs licking his lips at me, and I wanted to spit in his face.

"Where am I at Church? I need to get to a hospital."

"You need to talk to me first, and I'll think about it."

"You did all of this to talk?"

"No, I did all this because you broke my fucking heart Ki! You left me over some dumb shit." I can't believe he fixed his mouth to say that shit to me.

"No, I left because you cheated on me, and probably been cheating the entire relationship."

"It was one fucking person! You act like it's been a million bitches!"

"Right, it was just one bitch a million times which is worse!!"

Church slammed his fist against the dresser, and the mirror broke making a loud crashing sound that had me jumping out of my skin. After he knocked my ass out, I didn't want him to hit me ever again. He stood up and walked back toward the stairs.

"Where are you going? I can't stay down here Church, please just let me go home. This is crazy."

"Nah, when you change yo mind about being with me, then I'll let you out of here." The door slammed and I let out a loud ugly cry. I felt the urge to throw up so I got out the bed, and spotted a small half bathroom down here.

I was throwing up what felt like poison, and my body was drained. I hope I don't lose my baby down here, Church would have to kill me then, because I wouldn't rest until he took his last breath. I don't understand how someone I used to be so in love with could do me like this. He is seriously punishing me because I don't want to be with him. I really hope Deontae came looking for me, I know he probably think I ran again. I was so stupid for leaving out his house that night.

I pulled myself off the floor and drunk some water out of the bathroom faucet. I laid back in the bed and said a silent prayer that somebody would be here soon.

***

I laid in this bed counting down every hour that I was in this shitty ass basement. So far, I saw the sun rise two times, and I still haven't had anything to eat. But, that didn't stop me from throwing up all day. My baby was punishing me already, I really hope this don't continue through the entire pregnancy. As I was walking back to the bed Church came down and sat at the edge of the bed.

"What's it gone be? I know you hungry, it's been a few days."

I didn't acknowledge him as my mind drifted off to Deontae and I wondered if he was thinking about me. I swear I was missing his sexy chocolate ass, I just wanted to lay with him while he rubbed his fingers through my hair.

"Aite, suit yourself… I'll be back."

Church got up and went back upstairs. I swear he's lucky it's nothing I can use down here to stick in his throat because I'll do it without a second thought

My eyes started to get heavy, and I gave up fighting it and drifted off to sleep again.

Please God, let someone find me soon.

FIVE

Church

I didn't think it was gon' take Kiarra's tough ass this long to get her shit together. I puffed on my *Black & Mild*, and sat back on the couch to think of a plan. I had gotten a few calls saying Law was back in town, and looking for me, so I knew I was going to seeing him real soon. Law was a real OG and I knew the type of nigga he was and how he handled shit. I was ready for whatever, but I wasn't gone be the only nigga dead if that's the route he wanted to take.

My phone rang and snapped me out of my thoughts.

"Yoooo! Where you been my nigga?" It was one of my old homies Gates from back in my corner boy days.

"I'm chillin wassup, fuck you yelling for?"

"Shiiiit me and my girl finally back in town, I was trying to slide on you."

"That's cool I'll send you my location bro."

I hung up and texted him the address to where I was. He responded back saying he was twenty minutes away, so I straighten up the living room and lit another cigar.

When I saw an unknown car pull up in the driveway, my heart was beating fast as hell as I gripped my pistol. But, when I heard Gates loud as voice I put my gun up and opened the front door.

"Wassup bro, I see niggas got they jerry curls going on at the top, ol pretty boy ass nigga."

"Yo big ass always talking shit." Gates was a big burly ass nigga, and he was the type of nigga who always hit you when they laughed. I be ready to knock his ass out.

"You know I'm fucking with ya bro. Aw shit my bad, this my girl Kodi, Kodi this my bro Church."

"Hey, how you doing?" Her head was in her phone and she didn't even bother looking up. Gates smacked her phone on the floor and kicked it across the room when she tried to pick it up.

"Oh my God that's so childish, but it's cool, you gon' be buying me another one."

It seemed like they was about to be on some arguing shit so I excused myself, and told them I'll be back.

Miranda had been blowing my phone up, and I been ignoring that shit. She was due any day now, and I figured I missed the birth or something. I left out the house and drove to the house we shared. The second my foot stepped over the threshold she started with her shit.

"Church really! My freaking water broke because I was worried something happened to you! Some people stopped by looking for you talking about Kiarra is missing. Did you do something to her?"

"Didn't you just say your water just broke? Shut the fuck up and come on damn, you worried bout the wrong shit." I forgot I had Kiarra ass in the basement, I hope Gates and his girl don't take they nosey ass down there.

I walked back outside and sat in the car. Miranda came scurrying outside a few minutes later and I finally noticed Mia wasn't with her.

"Where my baby girl at?"

"My mama came and got her yesterday, not like you care."

"Aw ok."

We rode in silence to the hospital, aside from Miranda doing her deep breathing in the passenger seat. I feel kind of fucked up, I should be focusing on my girl, but I couldn't get Kiarra off my mind. I didn't mean to hurt Kiarra, but I meant when I told her that nigga would never have her. I'll have her burying him first... or him burying her.

I drove to the hospital and I was on full alert making sure I wasn't being followed. I took her to *Little Company of Mary*, because it was far enough away, and I didn't think people would spot me out here.

"I can't believe you drove all the way out here. What's going on Church, you need to tell me something?"

"I don't need to tell you shit, you need to act like a fucking man and grow!"

Smack!

She smacked hard as fuck across my face, and I was ready to headbutt her ass.

"Keep your hands to yourself Miranda, that's my last warning."

"Fuck you and your warning! You don't care about

me or my feelings so bit—"

Smack!

"I told you to keep your fucking hands off of me!"

"Why would you hit me, I'm over here pregnant, and you just hit me?" She was crying and being dramatic, and I barely touched her ass.

"You talk too fucking much, I'm tired of that shit. Get the fuck out the car and go have my son."

"Are you at least coming in?" Her waterworks came to a halt fast as she was back to staring at me with an attitude.

"Yeah man… come the fuck on."

Miranda wiped the fake ass tears from her face and waddled in the hospital. I pulled my hood over my head before I walked in behind her. She was rushed right up to a labor and delivery room, and hooked up to a monitor.

"Ok, you're about 6 centimeters, so baby should be here soon. How's your pain, on a scale of 1 to 10?"

"It's about a 5, I'm ok."

"Ok, page us if you need something."

The nurse walked out the room, and I got comfortable in my seat. When she had Mia, she was loud and dramatic, wanting me to be right next to her, now she was acting distant and acting like I wasn't here. I know she wasn't mad 'cuz I smacked her, shit she hit my ass first.

"What's yo problem?"

"Nothing." She rolled her eyes and stared up at the tv.

"Speak the fuck up 'cuz I don't wanna hear shit later."

"Why do you treat me like this? I didn't do nothing but love you, and you act like I'm still not good enough. It is because I'm not Kiarra?"

"Man, you forced yourself into my life, so don't blame me for it not being all fucking sprinkles and fairy dust like you imagined it to be. You knew I had a girl, and you still kept trying shit."

"Yeah, but you been climbing in my bed every chance you get, I didn't do the shit alone."

"Hell naw I aint turning down no easy pussy. What the fuck is you even complaining about g?"

"Forget it Marshall, we can never have a real conversation without you getting like that. Ooowww." She held her stomach, and start doing her deep breathing.

When it was time for her to push, I stood up and watched my son come into the world. I had doubts that he was mine, but when I stared at him he looked just like Mia. They got him cleaned up and I sat in the rocking chair holding him and stared into his eyes that mirrored mine. I know I was fucked up for what I did to Kiarra, I honestly don't know why I did it. Miranda was cool, when she wasn't complaining about shit, but like she said... she wasn't Kiarra.

Kiarra was everything I wanted and more. I know you probably thinking why I aint just get my shit together sooner? Well I don't fucking know. I aint think the shit was gone come back on me like this though.

"Can I get some time with my son Church?" I handed him to her and sat back down. I watched how Miranda was with him, and it made me regret putting my hands on her; especially since she was still carrying my son.

Tre was right, I need to get my shit together.

SIX

Kiarra

I was in a nice slumber when I heard a guy talking loud as hell. It scared the hell out of me because I thought he was standing right over me, but he was all the way upstairs. I walked to the bathroom again and drunk some water out of the sink. I looked around for a way out of here, but all I saw were some windows. I knew I wasn't climbing my ass out of a window, I mean I had been working out with Tae, but I wasn't on that level yet.

The basement door opened and a short light skin girl came downstairs. "Oh, I'm sorry, I was looking for a bathroom can I use that one?"

"Yeah go ahead." I sat back on the edge of the bed, and tried to listen for footsteps upstairs. I only heard one set but he sounded big as hell. I wasn't about to risk my baby fighting a damn bear.

The girl came back out the bathroom drying her hands on a paper towel and sat down on the ottoman across from me.

This heffa getting real comfortable.

"I'm Kodi, sorry I didn't introduce myself before I used your bathroom."

"It's cool, so whose all upstairs?

"Just Gates… Church left a little while ago, he didn't even say anybody was here."

"Oh, uh… do you have a phone I could use?"

"Yeah, that dummy just cracked my screen but it works just fine." I grabbed my bag I saw sitting on the floor and pulled my debit card out to order an Uber. This nigga had me all the way in Gary, Indiana and it was about to cost me over a hundred dollars but I didn't care.

I saw that my ride was arriving, so I put my shoes on and grabbed my bag.

"Here you go, thanks for that."

"You leaving? Dang I thought I had a friend." I felt awkward as I stood there looking at her.

"Um... sorry, just tell Church I'll be back." I walked up the stairs quickly and saw this big guy laid across the couch. He snoring so loud you would've thought it was a lion roaring in here.

I ran outside and got in my waiting Uber before I let out a sigh of relief. I gave the guy a $50 tip just for coming so fast, and he put the address in his gps. The ride back to the city was about 45 minutes, and I just hope it wasn't any traffic.

I dozed off and woke up to the Uber driver tapping on my leg. "I didn't mean to invade yo space, but you're here miss."

"It's ok, I didn't even mean to fall asleep, thank you again." I got out the car and walked into Deontae's building.

I went up to his door and knocked a few times. There was no answer, and I didn't hear any movement inside so I knocked a little louder in case he was sleep. Still no answer. I sat on the floor against his door and waited until he got home... hopefully I'm not here all night, because I don't have a cellphone to get another ride.

SEVEN

Deontae

It had been a few days since Kiarra disappeared and I had been out every day looking for any sign of her. It was after 9 at night, and I was finally going home after having no luck. My mom had been calling me all day, and I was ignoring her. Well I been ignoring her since the night Kiarra ran out the house. I didn't want to worry her about what was going on until we had everything under control.

I pulled into my parking garage, and grabbed my Popeyes from the passenger seat before I got out my truck. When I got off the elevator on my floor, I saw someone sleep in front of my door. When I got closer I dropped my food and ran to her.

"Ki? Ki baby wake up." She opened her eyes and smiled at me.

"It took you long enough, I thought I was going to be out here all night."

"Are you ok? Should we go to the hospital? How did you get here?"

"No, I'm fine, can you start by unlocking the door?"

"My bad, come on."

"I'm mad you wasted that Popeyes like that, it smells so good."

"You want me to go get some more?" I picked the garbage up while she held the door open for me. When I locked the door, I grabbed her and held on tight to her."

"I'm so sorry Tae, I shouldn't have left, it was so stupid."

"Baby girl, you don't have to apologize, I'm just happy you're ok. Let me check your head though."

"I think I got a concussion, I been falling asleep everywhere."

I got the small gash on her forehead cleaned, and ran her some bath water. The rest of the night was spent with me taking care of her, and I wouldn't have it any other way. When she fell asleep, I stepped out to the living room and called Kiarra's mom.

"Hello?"

"Hey, how are you doing Mrs. Walker?"

"I'm ok, Deontae, what's going on?"

"I found Kiarra, or she found me… she's here at my house, but she's sleeping. If you want, I can send you my address in the morning and you can come, I just want her to get some rest."

"I understand, well you take care of my bay, and I'll call and let everyone know, see you tomorrow Deontae, thank you."

She hung up, and I made sure the door was locked before I shut all the lights out. I went to take me a long hot shower, and I swear it felt like I was washing all my stress away. Once I washed up a few times, I stepped out the shower and wrapped my towel around my waist. Kiarra was sitting up in the bed like she wasn't just sleep 10 minutes ago.

"What's wrong, you feeling ok why you get up?"

"My head is hurting a little bit; do you have some regular strength Tylenol?"

"Naw, but I can go run and get some."

"No, you just got out the shower, I'll be ok."

"Come on Ki, let me take care of you. and I spoke with your mom, she said everyone will be here tomorrow."

"Ok, that's fine. Can you just rub my scalp until I fall back asleep bae?"

I put on my boxers, and got in the bed behind her. Kiarra laid on my chest, and I rubbed her scalp until I heard her light snoring. I couldn't sleep as I held on to her and thanked the Man upstairs that she was back in my arms.

*****

Kiarra was tossing and turning all night, and I barely got any sleep. When she got up the next morning, she took another shower, and I rubbed her feet while we watched tv and waited for everyone to show up.

"Kiarra I think you should go see someone."

"Someone like who?"

"A counselor, to talk about what you just went through. You tossed and turned all night, and woke up drenched in sweat."

"It was one night Deontae really? If you want to

sleep peacefully, I'll go home or to Lo's house."

"I'm just trying to look out for you."

"As a doctor or my man?"

"Both Kiarra, don't fight me on this." I heard knocks at the door so I got up to answer it.

Kiarra's mom walked in, followed by Lauren's parents, Lauren, and Banks.

"Good morning Deontae, I brought stuff to make breakfast, where's Kiarra?"

"Good morning Mrs. Walker, she's in the back I'll go get her."

"No, I'll do it, just point me in the right direction. This is a nice place you have here too."

"Thank you." I showed her where my room was and all the women walked back there.

"We gone be waiting for a minute, you got some beer? What channel is ESPN on the box in here?" Lauren's father took his jacket off and got comfortable on the couch. I mean he really got comfortable, my mans took his shoes off and laid down.

They better hurry up back there.

EIGHT

Kiarra

When Deontae walked out the room I wanted to chase behind him and defend myself, but I didn't have the energy. I heard footsteps coming down the hall and my mom, Lauren, and Aunt Steph walked into the room. Lauren ran to me first and almost knocked me out the bed.

"Girl! Don't let nobody snatch you up no more, had me all worried and shit."

"Really Lo, it's not like I asked him to knock me the hell out and take me. Do you see my damn face?"

"Girl bye, I'll send Gio downstairs to get my make-up bag, and you wouldn't see nothing."

"Um hello… Kiarra's mother would like to get in here and get a hug."

"Sorry ma." Lauren laughed and scooted over so my mom could get in by me.

"Hey Chubbz, you scared ne half to death, my stomach was messed up I had the nervous shits. Do you know how uncomfortable that is?"

"Maaaa, come on I don't wanna hear that."

"That's too bad, you heard it already. Speaking of something that's been heard; I hear I have a grand baby on the way." I couldn't help the smile when she mentioned my baby.

"Yeah, I'm excited, I hope I have a boy, I don't think I can handle the attitudes, and everything else that comes with having a daughter. But I think if it was a girl she'll be my little mini."

"I don't know, I seen Deontae's father, and it look like he chewed him up and spit him out by himself."

"But I look just like daddy."

"Yeaaaahh, well we'll see boo boo." I missed having these times with my mom, I hope she stay a while this time.

"Y'all come on out so we can eat shit, I'm hungry!"

"Law shut the hell up, wasn't you eating in the car?"

"Mind yo bidness Mel, stay in yo own car." We laughed and I followed everyone out to the living room, I hugged Aunt Steph before Uncle Law was snatching me up and putting me in a bear hug.

"I'm glad you ok Ki, I would've felt like shit if I didn't keep my promise to Ken."

"Don't think like that Uncle Law, you do more than enough for me."

"I aint talking about finiancially, I promised him I'll protect you. Where at nigga Church at now?"

"I don't want to talk about that right now. Let's just enjoy this time together, I haven't seen all my family together in a while."

"You got that, but I'm not done."

I just shook my head and sat on the couch. Call me crazy but I didn't want Church killed, at the end of the day he has kids to live for. And with my own on the way, I can't be the reason a child is fatherless.

My mom and Aunt Steph cooked breakfast while everyone else sat bac watching the NBA games that were on. Deontae kept asking me every 5 minutes if I was ok, and I was starting to get irritated. Lauren noticed me roll my eyes at Tae and she shook her head at me.

"Ki, come here right quick." She stood up and walked back towards the bedroom. I got up and followed her, and closed the door behind me.

"What I do now Lauren?"

"Why are you getting mad at that man?"

"I'm not mad at nobody, what you talking about?"

"Yeah ok, you better get yo life together. When are you going to check on the baby?"

"I'll go to the hospital Monday, I gotta go talk to my boss anyway… hope I still got a damn job."

"I think Deontae told them something already, you need to talk to him. Stop being so damn stubborn."

There was a knock at the door, and Deontae poked his head in. "The food ready when y'all done."

"Here we come Tae." He gave me a look before he walked out.

"You better get yourself together before you run him away."

Lauren followed me back out to the front of the house and I sat at the island to eat my food. When Deontae sat next to me, I gave him a kiss on the cheek and finished eating.

*****

Monday morning rolled around and Tae got up so he could leave for work. I was leaving with him because I promised to see about the baby.

"Come find me when you done baby girl."

"Ok, have a good day."

I walked down to my boss's office and saw her sitting behind her desk, so I knocked and walked in.

"Heeyyy, how are you feeling? I heard about the accident are you ok?"

"Yeah, I'm fine, I was just stopping by to let you know I'll be taking another two weeks off… I'm still in a lot of pain."

"That's fine honey, take all the time you need, I'll see you when you come back."

I walked out her office and ran right into Kim.

"Do you wanna tell me why you been ignoring my calls?"

"I haven't, my phone is broke, I just haven't had the time to go replace it."

"Ok… so how are you feeling?"

"I'm fine, I'm on my way to my appointment now."

"I'll walk with you, I'm on break." She followed me on the elevator and I wanted to tell her to go find some business, but I wasn't gone be rude. "Girl you missed some tea the other day."

"Kim, I'm not really in the mood for gossip, I'm trying not to throw up in this elevator." The elevator stopped and I got off with Kim following me to the OB/GYN's off. She grabbed my hand and stopped me from walking inside.

"Are you pregnant?"

"Is that the only reason people come here?"

"I mean yeah, so are you?"

"You nosey as hell Kim you know that?"

"But you love me so it's ok. I'm happy for you though, now Miles and Mila will have another friend to play with. Let me go back up before I'm being paged... congratulations boo."

"Thank you." she hugged me and walked to the elevator.

I signed in at the front desk and waited to be seen. My appointment went fast and I found out I was due on Halloween. I'm so glad everything with the baby is ok, and I know Deontae is going to be ok.

I got my ultrasound pictures and stuffed them in my purse before I went back upstairs to tell Deontae I was leaving. As soon as I stepped off the elevator, I ran into Dr. Pierce, another surgeon at the hospital.

"Hey Nurse Kiarra, we miss you up here."

"I promise I'll be back soon. Have you seen Dr. Blak?"

"He was scrubbing up in OR 3 to help with a guy who was vomiting blood... go up to the dock and check it out."

Now, some people would've ran the other way, but I went right to the sitting area that was overlooking OR 3 and got a seat right in front. Deontae had just walked in and I kept my eyes trained on him.

Through the entire surgery his facial expression didn't change. It was like a totally different person than the smiling Deontae I usually saw. His face was stone cold, but focused; I'm surprised he could hear what was going on around him.

When I see him like this it made me fall in love with him even more. I know our child will be proud to call him dad.

I waited until he was done with his surgery so I could show him the pictures.

"What you still doing here? I thought you would've went to the house by now."

"No, I was watching you work, and I wanted to show you the little alien in my stomach." I pulled the ultrasound pictures out of my purse and his face lit up.

"Damn Ki, this shit dope, I can't wait to see his or her face."

"I hope it's a him, I don't think I can deal with all the attitude that comes with having a daughter.

"Oh, you scared she might act just like you huh?"

"And what's wrong with the way I act Dr. Blak?"

"Nothing baby, I'll take an Uber home, so you can take my car. You staying at my place, right?"

"Yeah, I'll be there until I can come back to work." He gave me a quick kiss and I left out the door.

Some of the staff was staring at me, I guess because it was the first time me and Deontae ever showed affection at work, but oh well… we were about to share a whole baby.

When I got in the car I called Mama Roxy, and she answered on the first ring.

"I was about to come lay hands on you and that son of mine, why the hell nobody been answering the phone?"

"It's been crazy with work, I'm sorry… I'm off now if you want to go make up for our missed time."

"Yeah come on by, I'm just watching my shows."

"Ok, I'm on my way." I drove to Deontae's parents' house in Richton Park, and made sure to grab the sonogram pictures I had. I know if I showed her these right off bat, she won't cuss me out too bad.

NINE

Lauren

Now that Ki was home safe I had to get back to work. People was messaging me asking for pictures like I don't have a life outside of this. Especially since I been working to get my studio open.

I took a break from my editing to call Gio since I missed his call earlier, and he answered on the first ring.

"What you doing tomorrow bae?"

"That is not how you answer the phone."

"My bad, for real though what you doing tomorrow?"

"Nothing, I was going to go sit with Ki, she been bored in the house."

"You gotta do that another day, I need you downtown with me tomorrow."

"Okaaayyy? I need more details then that. What am I doing? Whose going to be there? How early do I gotta wake up?"

"It's a video shoot--"

"What the hell that mean I gotta be up early as hell. It aint looking good for you."

"I need my leading lady Lo, you getting a free hairstyle, and you can keep whatever clothes you want."

"You should've started with that, what time you gone be here?"

"I'll be there by 5, just throw on some sweats."

"At 5 in the damn morning, you better be lucky I don't come out in my pajamas."

"Bye Lo, I gotta get back in the booth, love you."

"Love you too."

Kiarra was gon' be mad, but I can't turn now money, and free clothes.

Don't hate me

Huuuuhhh you not coming, are you?

I'll come after I get done with this shoot I promise

Fine... I'm going back to sleep

***

When Gio came ringing my bell at 5 in the morning I had a fit. I am not a morning person at all, and stomped around my apartment the entire time I was getting ready.

But, when we walked onto his set and I got my hair slaaayyyed hunty... this became my video, just call me David Ruffin.

I walked out my dressing room with my robe on, strutting like I was on the runway and Gio just shook his head at me.

"Girl you better chill out, you about to be in all of three scenes."

"And these gon' be the best 3 scenes of yo video."

"I know bae, 'cause yo sexy ass in it."

"You still paying me, so don't think your sweet talking is moving me, nice try though."

I didn't finish wrapping up my part of the shoot until 3 in the afternoon; so I took an Uber to Kiarra's house and stayed there until Deontae came home from work.

One thing I never had to worry about Deontae loving Kiarra. I can tell by the way he looked at her that he would lay down for her.

When I got home I had to take a long bath with my glass of wine and cigarette. Gio hated when I smoked, so I had my pack hidden whenever he came over here.

I stepped out the tub when I heard my phone ringing and saw it was a missed call from the contractor installing the green screens in my studio. I called him back as I dried off and slipped into one of my Victoria Secret.

"This is Miguel."

"Hey Mike, this Lauren, you just called me?"

"I keep telling you my name is Miguel."

"Yeah… but you black so I think yo mama meant to name you Mike."

"Anyways, I called because there's a problem with one of the screens… it doesn't fit."

"What do you mean it don't fit?"

"It doesn't cover the entire wall behind it, so if you record something, that spot is going stick out like a sore thumb."

"Ok so get a bigger screen."

"It's going to take 3 weeks to get the screen in, apparently they're real popular right now." I wanted to scream and have a fit but I just did some deep breathing until I got off the phone.

"Ok, thank you Miguel just let me know if there's any way I could get it earlier."

"Alright Ms. Lauren, how about I stop by and--."

Click

He started getting his suave voice on, and I aint got time to be fighting Banks crazy ass.

My social media followers went up so I start posting about free shoots, and I had been getting a lot of responds back. I guess my prices were too high, or people were just cheap as hell, because the second I mention some free shit, people start flocking.

As long as it brings in some new business then I'm good with it.

TEN

Kodi

I was waiting on my time to shine, because I got a story to tell. First off, I'm Kodi... no last name like Cher. I'm 25 years old, and I can't say I did much with my life, except follow my boyfriend Gates around for the last 7 years.

When we first got together, he was a petty hustler, selling nickel and dime bags while he stayed in his mother's basement.

But I didn't care about none of that, I stayed right in that stuffy ass basement with him, sharing meals from McDonalds, and washing our clothes by hand in the tub.

He just kept telling me stay down for him and it's all gone play off in the end. But, 7 years later and all I got was my ass beat for breakfast, lunch, and dinner, and sometime a midnight snack. The only body part he couldn't keep to himself, was his dick; I lost count of the many bitches he had cheated on me with.

He did spoil me financially, but I'll rather go back to struggling in his mama's basement; at least then I didn't have to buy a shit load of concealer to cover all my bruises.

When we got back to Illinois, after living in Iowa for the last 3 years, Gates told me he was done cheating, and putting his hands on me, but that lasted all of a week.

When I confronted him about some texts from a chick he was planning to meet up with, he beat my ass and left me on the floor in our new townhouse for the whole day. I knew I had a fractured rib or 2, but I sucked all that pain up and went shopping when he handed me a book bag full of money. I'm not dumb, I know he came out here to start selling dope with Church and Tre again. But what can I do about it?

I took Gates car and drove to State street and parked in a garage. All of the stores I wanted to go in were on this street, so I was just going to walk. Going into *A'Gaci* first, I went through every rack grabbing anything I thought was cute.

Shopping is my therapy for real. When you're forced to deal with the monster I had to every day, you value all time you have outside away from it. Some days were good, and he treated me like he actually cared

My sisters told me I should leave him after the first time he went upside my head, but like the love sick puppy I am…I went right back. What people fail to realize is that Gates wasn't always like this. The man I fell in love with was always sensitive towards my feelings, and actually valued our relationship. Now, it's like he doesn't want me, but he doesn't want to let me go either. The one time I did find the strength to leave him, he popped up on me and beat my ass so bad, I couldn't recognize myself in the mirror. I had to stay hidden for almost a month until all of the bruises were gone.

Silly of me to think he was finally going to grow up.

"Hey are you ok?"

I looked up and saw the girl that was in Church's basement a few weeks ago. She handed me a piece of tissue and I wipes away the tears I didn't even know were falling.

"I'm fine, thanks for that."

"You look familiar."

"I'm Kodi… I met you at Church house that day in the basement."

She started looking uncomfortable and looked over her shoulder. "That's right, I'm Kiarra, don't tell him you saw me ok?"

The way she was looking around had me wondering if she was dealing with the same shit I was. You know they say birds of a feather flock together.

"Take my number down, if you ever need someone to talk to, don't hesitate to give me a call. This baby have me up all times of night anyway."

"Aww congrats, you don't even look pregnant." It was true, her stomach was still flat and she had on a crop that exposed her tummy.

"It's still early, I hope I don't blow up too much."

"Is it Church baby? I heard him talking about his son."

"Girl, hell naw, me and Church been broken up for a while, for that exact reason."

Gates started calling me, so I walked towards the counter to pay for my stuff. "Thanks again, and I'll be hitting yo line soon."

"No problem, take care of yourself."

She went back to shopping as the cashier was ringing my clothes up. I rushed out the store and to the car so I can hurry up and get back. When I walked in the house Gates was sitting on the couch rolling a blunt.

"You aint waste no time going shopping I see."

"Naw, I was bored, so I did a little bit, what do you

want for dinner."

"I don't know, you wanna go out tonight?" I looked shocked at him and looked around the house.

"What you looking for?"

"I don't know the cameras or something, this gotta be some kind of sick prank or something."

"Damn, I can't take my girl out?"

I wanted to ask him which girl was he talking about because he haven't taken me anywhere but to the hospital in last few years.

"Where do you want to go Gates?"

"I don't know, it don't matter, anywhere you want to go."

I saw a place earlier I wanted to check out, but I knew he wasn't gone go for that. "Anywhere I want to go you're going to go with me?"

"Yeah, what you got in mind?"

"Paint & Sip."

"You tweaking KoKo, what I look like taking my big ass in there?"

"Well you said anywhere I want to go."

"Aite, you got that. I'll be back by 6 so by ready to go."

"Where you going?" The question left my mouth before I could even stop myself, and I just knew I was about to be picking my teeth up off the floor.

"I gotta handle some business, I'll be back bae."

He kissed me before he left out the door, and I sat trying to wake myself up from the dream I was in.

Instead of wasting time, I got up to prep myself for tonight. I showered, washed my hair and put my flexi rods in so it could be cute and curly. As I was finding the perfect outfit, I got a glimpse of the big purple bruise that was on my side, compliments of Gates getting caught cheating again. I laid down and cried myself to sleep.

"Kodi!"

"Hmmm?"

"I thought I told you to be ready, you laying here not even dressed."

"I'm not in the mood to go out anymore, I'm not feeling good." I sat up in the bed and he looked me up and down.

"Man stop playing, after all the complaining you did about me not doing shit with you, you better get the fuck up!"

He raised his voice but I didn't flinch this time. "I don't feel like going. My ribs are hurting, I'm not in the mood to fake my pain tonight. Ahh!" Gate punched me in the face and I fell back onto to the bed.

"You just love opening that mouth of yours, don't you? why you couldn't just take this good gesture and act right for once? Huh?" he spoke between every punch he landed on my body. When he pulled me out the bed by my ankle, I hit the hardwood making a loud thud and

"Ok Gates! Please stop, I'm sorry, just please stop." I was balled up in the fetal position as he stomped me with his Timberland boots on.

"I'm bout to go take a more grateful bitch out, you can sit yo ass in the house and clean this shit up."

He walked out the room, and out the house, as I laid on the floor coughing up blood. I pulled myself up and went into the bathroom. When I saw the new damage to my face, I felt defeated. I just wanted to end it all, I didn't deserve to live like this.

My nose was twisted and bleeding, and I knew it was broken because I could barely breathe through it. I went to the walk in closet, and grabbed a duffle bag. Moving as fast as I could, I threw a bunch of clothes in it and grabbed my phone. I didn't have any family close because they all stayed in Lafayette, Indiana... so I called the only other person I knew in Chicago.

"Hello?"

"Hey Kiarra, it's Kodi, are you busy?"

"Hey girl! and not really, I'm waiting on my boyfriend to get off, wassup?"

"I need a ride, like right now."

"Send me your address."

"Ok, thank you so much." I hung up the phone and sent her my location.

I hope she made it here before Gates came back, I don't even wanna know what he was going to do if he saw me trying to leave again.

ELEVEN

Kiarra

When I got a call from an unknown number, I almost didn't answer, but something told me to do it anyway. It was something in Kodi's eyes when I saw her that screamed help, and I wanted to help her like she helped me get away from Church,

Speaking of Church, I'm surprised he haven't popped up anywhere yet. I had to beg Uncle Law not to kill him and go back to Miami, and trust me it wasn't easy.

My phone chimed, and Kodi sent me an address that was in the heart of Englewood, and I ha. She was driving a nice ass car when I saw her earlier, so I don't know why the hell they were in the hood. I was definitely bringing my gun with me going over there.

I hopped in my Infiniti truck and followed my gps to a house on 69th and Paulina. I texted her when I was a block away to come outside, and she as standing on the curb when I pulled up. Kodi put her bag in the trunk and got in the car. Right away I saw the bruises and twisted nose that she tried to hide behind her glasses and hair.

"OHMIGOD! Did he do that to you? Is his bitch ass still in there?" I put the truck in park and grabbed my gun from the arm rest When I was taking off my seatbelt she grabbed my arm.

"No he's gone, please just hurry before he gets back."

"Ok, I'll take you to my job to get checked out,

where are you going to go because you're not going back there."

"I don't know, my family is all in Indiana, but I don't really wanna go back there to the I told you so's."

"You stay in my apartment as long as you want, my boyfriend don't want me to leave his house since Church snatched me, so I'm never there."

"Wait, what you mean he snatched you?"

"Like gun to my head, fist to my face snatched my ass up. That's why I was in that basement, now I feel like God did it so that meet you and repay the favor. I just have one condition though."

"What's that?"

"Don't let anyone know where I stay, and please don't go back to him."

"That was two things."

"Well, I have two damn conditions." She laughed we rode to the hospital listening to the radio. I texted Deontae and let him I was on my way up there and he texted me back right away.

Are you ok, what's going on?

I'm fine, it's my friend, she's beat up pretty bad.

Ok, I'll try to see you when you get here, just had a trauma come in.

Love you have a great surgery

Love you more

"That must be your boyfriend, I remember when I use to smile like that. Gates haven't always been like this. I think it's the money, it changes people."

I could definitely agree with that, I know when Church and Tre start making bigger moves, that's when he started to change. And just like Kodi did, I ignored it… I'm glad I got out of it before it ruined me completely. Even with that stunt he pulled a few weeks ago, I'm still going to live my life.

"You don't have to try to defend your decision to stay with him to me. When you think you love someone, you try your best to see the good in them, even when all they're showing is the ugly."

Kodi was crying in the passenger seat as I pulled into the parking garage of the hospital. "It's ok, you're going to be fine, and I got your back whenever you need me, we can get you a new phone, one he can't trace."

"I have a secret account, I can get all the cash out."

"Ok, wipe your face, and let's go in. You don't have to give names, just say you got jumped outside somewhere." I could get in a lot of trouble for this, but I know what type of stuff men like Gates was capable of if they knew you sent the police sniffing around them.

She asked me to wait with her so I sat in the room until they put her to sleep to put her nose back in place. Deontae had texted and said he said a few minutes between surgeries so I met him in the on call room.

"What's the matter Tae, you look stressed."

"Yeah, I lost my patient, he bled out too much, and we couldn't stop it in time."

"It's ok, it wasn't your fault."

"I mean it kind of is, it was my job to save him, and I couldn't."

"You been doing this for a while I'm sure this isn't the first patient you ever lost is it?"

"Yeah it is, I prided myself on never losing a patient… now what can I say?"

"You can say that you have a girlfriend that loves you very much, and baby that's going to love you even more. You are still a great doctor Deontae, don't let this kill your spirit." There was a knock at the door and Kim came in.

"Sorry guys, but Dr. Blak you're being paged down to OR 1, and Ki your friend is done, we're waiting on her to come to."

"Ok, here we come." Deontae kissed me, then bent down to kiss my stomach before we walked out of the room and went our separate ways.

Kodi was sleeping peacefully in her hospital bed, and I sat in the chair next to her and turned the tv on. I realized I haven't talked to Lo in a few hours so I called her to see if she was up.

"Hey boo thang, wassup?"

"Nothing, I was checking on you."

"I'm good, I aint doing nothing but going over these edits."

"Aaawww I should've known."

"What you doing, it sound like you at work?"

"I mean I am but I'm not working. Kodi's boyfriend beat her ass kinda bad."

"Kodi who? From the basement?"

"Yeah, we ran into each other earlier and I told her to call me if she wanted to talk."

"That's a real twisted friendship y'all got going on, but I'm glad you was there to help her. I can't stand a dude who beat on a female and think it's ok. I wish Gio would call himself tryna hit me… he'll think he back on the block the way imma air his crib out."

"You are a nut Lo."

"No, I'm dead serious, you know who my daddy is, I could get any gun known to man. I want him to try me, that's why Tre caught that tire iron upside the head, I felt like I was under attack."

"You always spinning the story on something, you was the one going through the house like a hurricane beating people ass and bussing out windows."

"Yeah, I was… but when he walked up on me, I felt like he was jumping me so I bucked first."

"You need help boo, but I'll leave you to your craziness, call me tomorrow. Love you."

"Love you too pumpkin."

Kodi didn't wake up until two hours later, but I was sitting there the entire time. I told Deontae that she was going to be staying at my place, and he got some sleep in the *On Call Room* while he waited on me.

"I thought you would've been going by the time I woke up."

"Naw, I told you I was staying, they said you can go after the medicine wear off."

"Thank you so much for this, I don't know how I could repay you." She had started to cry and I had to look away before I was crying too. This baby had me all discombobulated, I cried about everything, and I have no control over it.

"Don't mention it, just worry about taking care of yourself." I waited until she was discharged and drove her to my house while Deontae followed behind me.

"Your place is nice as hell, definitely better than the ghetto shack I was just in."

She took her shoes off and I showed her around.

"The fridge and cabinet is fully stocked, if you need anything just call me and I can get it or have it delivered for you."

"I'm fine, I just can't wait to get in that tub in there, it looks like it'll wash away all of my sins."

Ok, I'll leave you to it, I have a house phone that's for the alarm, but I'll call and check on you throughout the day. Good night and get some rest boo."

"Night."

Tae walked me to my truck and we rode the short distance to his place... or our place as he liked to remind me. I wouldn't mind officially moving in with him, there's more than enough room for us and the baby, it'll be smart.

We pulled into the parking garage, and Deontae came to open my door to help me out... and we walked in the building hand in hand.

"How you feeling baby girl, have you talked to your mom today?"

"I'm fine, and not really, I think she got a boyfriend and I don't know how to feel about this."

"Why, it's been a while since your father passed, don't you think she deserve to be happy too?"

"Uuuggghhh, I know... I just can't see her with nobody except my dad, it just won't feel right to me."

"You gotta have an open mind, what if she would've said she can't see you with nobody but Church?"

"Uh, no she'll never say that; he cheated on me multiple times, and had a kid on me... trust she'll rather have me alone than with him."

"Anyways... how well do you know this girl?"

"I don't really, I used her phone to get out of Church's house."

"What if she setting you up bae, that wasn't really smart."

"I'm sure nobody is going to beat their own ass, and break their nose, just to set somebody up."

"You don't know how the streets work Kiarra, motha fuckas go to the extreme to get something done."

"And how do you know how the streets work Dr. Blak."

"I wasn't born a damn doctor, while yo think you funny."

"I am kind of funny, don't be mad."

"Yeah ok, don't quit yo day job."

Deontae rubbed my feet as I got ready to go back to sleep. I had to be up at 6 for my shift at the hospital and it was already passed 2 in the morning.

When my alarm went off, Tae got up with me and got dressed in his running gear.

"I gotta get me a jog in then I'll see you up there,

call me if you need anything, and don't overwork yourself."

"Sir, yes sir, and you don't beat yourself up about yesterday; it's a brand new day bae."

"Alright, love you." He gave me a kiss, then kissed my stomach before he left out the door. That was something he did every time he was leaving. I can't wait to meet our little bundle of joy.

****

I was halfway through my shift, and I was ready to crawl back in my bed. Right now, I was scrubbed in with Dr. Pierce while he did a heart valve replacement, and I was unbelievably nauseous.

"You ok over there Nurse Kiarra, I know you're not getting squeamish?"

"No, I'm fine." The room started to spin and I felt like my insides were burning up. "Can someone grab this please?"

I handed my instrument off and ran out of the room. I start tearing the gown I had on, off when Deontae came rushing in.

"What happened Ki?"

"I'm hot… help me take this off."

"Did you take a break, maybe you should go home."

"No, I just needed some damn air Deontae, excuse me." He moved from in front of the sink so I could wash my hands. There was no words spoken as we walked out in the hall and to the white board.

I took my name off the top, and went to the cafeteria.

"You just not going to say anything?"

"No, I rather not."

He shook his head and turned back around. "I'll see you later."

Lauren's voice telling me not to run Deontae, was echoing through my head, but shit he was gone run me away. I think we both needed a break anyway.

The rest of my shift, I tried to avoid Deontae, and it worked until I was leaving and he jumped on the elevator with me, and had me pinned against the wall. For some body that had been running around the hospital all day, he was smelling good as hell.

"You still mad at me baby?"

"I'm not mad, just irritated… if I tell you I'm ok, then I need you to believe me."

"Come on, I'm just worried about you, and the baby Ki, you can't fault me for that." Deontae brought his lips down to mine and I forgot all about having an attitude.

I let out a low moan and felt his member jump in his scrubs. "You better stop before I be leaving with you."

"I'll be waiting for you to get off."

The elevator opened at the parking garage, and I got off while he stood in the doorway. "Be careful, and call me when you make it in. Love y'all."

"We love you too."

TWELVE

Lauren

The last few weeks I spent waiting for the studio to get done, was the worse, but thankfully everything is done. My first client wanted photoshoot for her hair and eyelash line… shit if the hair look good enough, I might buy me a few bundles.

"Hi, I'm Nicole, the owner of Cutiee Bundles, thanks for agreeing to work with me. I've seen a lot of your work and I was very impressed."

"Thanks, I appreciate the support… I was thinking about grabbing me some of these inches for my birthday."

"I have some on hand, just let me know."

She got started getting everyone together to pose, and it smelled like a damn hair salon in here, all the oil sheen and edge control being passed around like a communion plate.

Gio walked in the door and all eyes were on him… as always. It was something I had to get used to seeming as though he was in the spotlight now more than ever. I excused myself from the group, and met him at the waiting area.

"Yo ass don't never answer the damn phone, I was tryna see if you wanted some Jerk tacos."

"And you know I'm working." I gave him a quick kiss on his lips and looked in his empty hands. "Sooo where's my food at?"

"I didn't get it, shit I aint know if you was hungry or not."

"Why are you here then if you came empty handed? You know I'm not turning down no tacos."

"Damn I came to see my girl before I go head back to the studio, is that ok with you short shit?"

"Giovanni?"

He looked behind me like he saw a ghost, and I turned around to see my client Nicole walking up to us.

"Heyyy how you been?" Gio looked at me like he was looking for permission to speak, and I was looking at her tryna figure out who told her to come interrupting my conversation.

"I'm good Nicki."

"Oh, Nicki huh? How do y'all know each other *Giovanni*?"

"You don't have nothing to worry about, he's an ex, I was speaking."

"Believe me baby, I wasn't worried either way. I'll see you later Banks, let me wrap up in here."

Nicole looked like she wanted to say something but I walked away and got back to work. The faster I got done, the faster I can get these heffas out my studio before I change my mind about acting like I got some sense in here.

When everything was done, Nicole tried to make conversation with me, but I shooed her ass right out the door. Once this lens cover was on my camera, all that professional shit went out the window. and that "talk" could've went all the way left.

I was speeding to the recording studio where Banks was, and I was ready to run his head through a wall.

His producer saw me and smiled, but quickly turned around when he saw the mug on my face. Banks stepped out the booth and told everybody to step out for a minute.

"Why you come in here look liking that bae?"

"Because I feel like you got me fucked up. Where did that Nicole chick come from?"

"Don't start with that hot head shit, I aint talked to her in a few years, since my music started to take off. She said some shit to you or something?"

"Naw, I didn't give her a chance to. I'm gone tell you straight up… I aint getting my heart broke again, so you either gone be my last love or the first body I catch. The choice is ultimately yours." He sat back in the chair laughing, while I was still standing in my spot at the door.

"Aint nobody tryna break yo crazy ass heart. I aint got time to be thinking no other bitches. Yo ex nigga was dub, we aint cut from the same cloth remember that."

"Yeah ok… you remember what I said because I'm not giving anymore warnings."

"I got you baby girl. Can I get back to work now?"

"Yeah ok, I'll see you later."

He could take me as a joke all he wanted, but I'm dead serious about my heart.

THIRTEEN

Kodi

I spent a few weeks in Kiarra's house and it was nice and all, but it was nothing to do in there but eat and sleep; and I was tired of doing both.

I caught an Uber back home and thankfully Gates car wasn't outside. I don't know how he was going to react to me leaving but I hoping he was in a better more than the one he was in the last we saw each other.

Everything in the house still looked exactly the same, and it pissed me off that he probably haven't even been home to notice I called myself leaving him. I unpacked my clothes, and straightened up the mess that was in the house.

My body wasn't completely healed, but I felt a lot better than I did the week before.

I got started cooking dinner and I heard the front door slam. Gates walked in, with a woman on his arms and I had to stop and do a double take

"Where you been hiding at KoKo?"

"Really that's what you wanna talk about? How about we address the fact that you brought another bitch in our house!"

"Shut the fuck up and go finish cooking Kodi."

"No! How can you say you love me when you treat me like shit?"

"Um... I'm just going to leave, I don't want any problems."

"Yeah bitch you can just leave 'cause this is my house!"

"What did I just tell you?" He walked up to me slowly and I backed up against the fridge.

"Is that what you wanted? Who want me to beat yo ass in here? I'm tryna show you some mercy."

"No, who wants to get their ass beat? But you're going to do it anyway." I guess those were the magic words because Gates grabbed the pot I had on the stove and hit me with it.

"Aaahh!!" the steaming hot mashed potatoes burned my skin, as I tried to protect my face the best I could. I heard the pot hit the floor and felt the pain of his size 12 shoe on my back

Just when I felt my body giving up on me, I heard banging on the front door. "Chicago PD open the door!"

I heard the commotion of Gates being detained but my body was experiencing so much pain, I just laid on the floor until the medics came to get me.

They rushed me on the back of an ambulance and speed to the hospital.

"Ma'am, stay with me, we're getting you to the hospital can you tell me your name?" I tried to open my mouth, but nothing came out. All I could think is this was all my fault, if I would've just listened to Kiarra I wouldn't be in this predicament right now.

Everyone told me I should've left Gates when he put his hands on me the first time. Now I'm paying for it, I just hope I didn't have to pay for it with my life.

The ambulance rushed me to Christ Hospital and I was wheeled right away to an operating room. My skin still felt like it was on fire, but they gave me medicine to put me to sleep.

Loving a dope Boy is going to be the death of me…

THIRTEEN

Lauren

"Lo, come on you gon' make me late to my own show."

"Well, you should've gave me an early enough warning, and not run in here at the last minute asking if I want to go with you."

"Bro… I told you two weeks ago, what you talking about the last minute?"

"And you should've reminded me yesterday." I was dressed and applying my makeup to go to Banks' show at the *UIC Pavilion,* when he came in rushing me.

"Just bring yo ass on man."

"Don't talk to me like that or I'm staying here." I put my favorite *Ruby Woo* lipstick on, and stood up from my vanity.

"Bout time, the car just pulled up."

Since he wanted to act impatient, I moved slow as I grabbed my purse, cellphone, and keys.

The entire ride to the United Center, Banks was on his phone like he had an attitude; huffing and puffing and shit. When we got there, Banks was rushed off to do sound check, while I went back to his dressing room. As I was fixing my bang in the mirror there was a knock at the door.

"Hey Giovanni, I—Oh I didn't know you were going to be here." Nicole walked in looking like she was about to hit the runway or something. I'm not gone lie her outfit was cute, but I wasn't telling her ass that.

"And why wouldn't I be supporting MY man?"

"He just said that you were always busy, so I didn't know."

"Bitch you knew."

"Excuse me?"

"You're excused, and the door is right there."

"Look I don't want any problems, I was just coming to say good luck to him."

"He don't need yo luck, he's already lucky enough to have me… thanks though, and enjoy the show." She walked out the door, and I heard a lot of commotion in the hallway. Of course I got my nosey ass to see what was going on.

I opened the door and Gio was arguing with Nicole, but stopped when he saw me. "You good bae? I was just on my way in to check on."

"Yeah, I bet, I'm bout to go home."

"Come on Lo, don't act like that, I need you there in the crowd." Nicole snickered and I had to count to 1,000 before I had to stomp some sense into her ass. She clearly don't know me or what I'm capable of, but I will definitely give her what she looking for.

I ordered an Uber while I walked through the crowd and it was there by time I made it out.

Gio clearly have me fucked up, him and that cross eyed amazon he called an ex-girlfriend, that wanna pop up all of a sudden. He better stop acting

I had the Uber driver take me to a bar that was close to my house, and I had me a few drinks at the bar.

I was gone call Ki, but knowing how she been with this pregnancy, she was probably sleep already.

"You too beautiful to have yo face all balled up, let me buy you a drink."

"And you too old to be using them tired ass pickup lines, no thank you."

"You aint even that cute to be stuck up like that."

"And yet you're still standing here wasting my time and yours."

"Bit—"

"Ay my mans, move around." Tre walked up to my table and I rolled my eyes at him. I knew I should've went my ass home. "What you doing all that for, you don't miss me?"

"It's a no for me jack."

"Come on Lo baby, you had time to cool off and shit, you gone come back to daddy now?"

I let out a loud laugh that had all the patrons in the bar turning around to look at me. "That was funny, you should really be a comedian."

"I wasn't joking with yo ass, why you gotta flaunt this nigga around my city?"

"Because I'm grown as hell and do what I want. You didn't care when you was flaunting yo lil' dusty hoes around."

"Aite keep playing and imma pull a Church on yo ass."

"Try it if you want, and see if I don't light yo ass up. Now, since you came over here disturbing my peace, take care of my tab for me."

I left out the bar and walked the few blocks to my house. If my dad knew he'll probably drag me by hair kick and screaming.

Gio had been blowing my phone since I left the arena, and I just put it on silent while I got ready for bed. I told Gio I wasn't playing with him, now it's time for me to show him I'm not playing.

****

The next day my alarm woke me up, and I got dressed to meet Ki at the doctor. She's supposed to find out what she was having today, and I was the one who was responsible for keeping the results.

I had 100 missed calls and text from Gio, and I kept ignoring him as I got myself together and left out.

"I'm so proud of you bestie, I thought you was gone be late. How was the show?"

I sat in the waiting area with Kiarra and Tae and he was giving me the side eye. I guess he talked to his cousin.

"I don't know I left before I had to stomp a mud hole in his ex's ass."

"Oh Lord what did she do?"

"Absolutely nothing, she just tried me a little bit. Don't look like that Ki, I didn't do anything either... I politely removed myself from that situation and went home."

"Kiarra Walker?"

The ultrasound technician lead us to the private room and Ki eagerly laid on the table.

"You're not finding out what you're having right?

"No, just tell her please."

The appointment went by fast, and we were out the door in no time.

Mama Melissa booked club *Aire* to have a Daytime Rooftop party for the gender reveal, and I thought it was a bit much for the occasion. But, this is her first grandbaby, and she's been away for a minute, so who am I to judge? I think she's tryna be slick and introduce Ki to her new man, but we will see, hope this don't ruin the day.

While everyone went to get dressed, I ran to Hobby Lobby to get the things I needed to announce baby Blak. I wanted to be extra and have Deontae cut it open from a mannequin or something, but Kiarra stomped on all my fun. But, I had another big surprise I put together for her so I didn't fight for it.

Gio was calling me AGAIN so I finally called him back when I went home to change into my party outfit.

"Hello?"

"Lauren, I swear you gone stop playing with me. Fuck you been at, I been calling you since last night?"

"I been around, but I'm busy getting this stuff together for the gender reveal what you need?"

"Imma need help getting my foot out yo ass if I gotta call yo egg head ass that many times again."

"Nah what you gone need is help getting my knife out yo neck if I have another encounter with that cock eyed ex bitch of yours."

I heard him laughing and I had to laugh too. "I told Tae her ass was cock eyed, his doctor ass talking about it's just lazy."

"Aint shit lazy bout that wanderer she got."

"Yo ass funny as hell. But for real bae, I aint thinking about her ass, you hear me?"

"Mmmhhmm. You coming to the party?"

"Yeah, I'm bout to be on my way up there."

"Come get me, I need help with this stuff."

"Bet, be there in 20."

I hung up and changed into my blue Team Boy baseball jersey I had made, and some jeans.

When Gio texted that he was outside, I grabbed everything I needed and left out the house. Today was a good day for me because this is going to be the second time I showed up somewhere on time.

The club was closed because it was a Sunday, but the manager was there to let us in. Melissa had the whole rooftop decorated with gold decorations everywhere, even the table covers were gold.

"Hey Ma, y'all got it real royal out here, it looks good though."

"Thank you, I want to introduce y'all to my friend Vince. Vince this my God daughter Lauren, and her guy Banks."

"Nice to meet you Vince." I smiled and shook his head, while I looked him up and down. Mama Mel was getting her groove back for real. Vince had to be at least 6ft, and had a James Harden beard. I had to do a double take on the slick at this dark skin eye candy. He had me ready to get rid of Gio's bright ass and come to the dark side.

"Lo don't make me clap yo ears together."

"What you talking bout bae?"

"I see the way you looking, get fucked up out here."

"Maaann bae I aint thinking about him." I mocked his voice and he muffed me before he went to grab a beer from the bartender.

My parents showed up next, and my mama had the same reaction I did when she saw Vince. But, the look my daddy was giving her had her looking away quick.

"Happy Father's Day daddy." I handed him the watch I bought him and gave him a kiss on the cheek.

"Thank you, Princess, where Ki at, I aint tryna be out here all day?"

"She should be on her way, go have a drink don't be irra tryna rush everybody."

Deontae's family took up most of the guests that was at the party, and everybody came with gifts. Imma make sure I remember all they faces, because if they show up empty handed to the baby shower, they won't be eating.

"They're on their way up everyone, make sure you all have you blue or pink pins, if you picked the right gender, we have prizes for everyone." Mama Mel was running around with these clothes pins acting like a crazy woman.

Deontae and Kiarra came to the rooftop and she started with the waterworks already.

This girl a damn crybaby.

FOURTEEN

Kiarra

Today was a special day for me, not only do I find out what I'm having, but it's Deontae's first unofficial Father's Day. He had been walking around the house smiling all morning, and saying how he couldn't wait to see what we were having.

When I walked into *Aire* and saw all of our family and friends, I start crying like a big baby.

"Come on bae we haven't even done anything yet and you crying." Deontae laughed and

"I know I can't help it, it's this baby." he rubbed my small baby bump and we walked around greeting everyone.

There was a table full of gifts, and I know the baby room was going to be cluttered with all the stuff we bought already.

"Hey Chubbz, how are you feeling sweetie?"

"I'm good ma, the morning sickness finally stopped, so I can enjoy my pregnancy." A tall dark skinned man walked up and I thought he was some kin of Deontae until he put his hand at the small of my mom's back.

"Kiarra and Deontae, let me introduce you to my friend Vince." He was smiling and held his hand out for me to shake. Deontae noticed my hesitation so he reached for it instead.

"Nice to meet you Vince, thanks for coming."

"No problem man."

My mom gave me the evil eye, so I just walked away to sit by Lauren.

"I can't believe she brought him here, like he family or something."

"He fine as hell, I'm glad she brought him shit. You better stop looking like that before yo mama come slap you upside down, you know Melanie don't play that, baby and all."

"I can't help it, you don't think it's too soon for her to move on? I mean she's still wearing her wedding ring and everything."

"Kiarra, it's been almost 10 years, how long is she supposed to wait?"

"I don't wanna talk about this, let's get this show on the road."

"Don't get an attitude with me because I don't agree with yo spoiled ass."

"You should be the last person to talk." Lauren stood up and went inside the club, while I went to speak to Deontae's parents who was at the bar.

"There go my daughter and law, I was wondering how long it was gone take you to get over here." His father spoke up firs

"Sorry, I got side tracked, how are two doing?"

"I'm good, I can't wait until my grandbaby get here, I'm going to steal her all the time just so you know."

"Please don't say her, I'm hoping this is a boy." Deontae joined us and added his two cent in on the conversation because he wanted a girl first, then a boy.

"Attention, attention can Ki and Tae please come to the front?" Lauren stood on a chair and was hitting a knife on one of the plastic champagne flutes from the table.

She pulled out a big black balloon that had question marks all over and handed it to Deontae.

"Ki, you pop the balloon, and put these goggles on before you be screaming about you can't see." Everyone laughed at her and I put the goggles on.

"On the count of three, 1….2….3."

The balloon popped and pink confetti went everywhere. I dropped my head and Deontae wrapped his arms around me as he laughed loudly in my ear. "Now I got my Queen and my Princess, don't be mad baby girl."

Everyone crowded us and I just smiled and held my tears in the best I could. Seeing all my family and friends around happy and celebrating—it makes me miss my daddy. I know he would've approved of Deontae, and he would've been the best grandfather ever.

The party resumed as people came to clean up the mess from the balloon.

"You ok bae?"

"Yeah, I'm getting tired, you know I didn't have my nap today."

"We can leave, go say bye to your mom." I cursed inwardly as my approached my mother and Vince sitting at a table.

"Hey, I'm getting ready to leave, I'll talk to you later ma, and it was nice meeting you Vince."

"Same here, congratulations on your baby girl." I gave him a tight lipped smile and my mama stood up to hug me.

"I'll call you in the morning Ki, I love you."

"Love you too ma."

I walked around saying bye to everyone as Tae and Banks put all the gifts in the trunk of Tae's trunk.

"I can't believe it's a girl, we need some boys in the family." Lauren said as she drank her glass of wine.

"Well you have some then."

"The devil is a liar, don't be speaking ill on me like that."

"Bye Lo, I'm not about to deal with yo foolishness,"

"Love you too."

Deontae came back to walk with me to the truck, and he helped me in.

"How you feeling baby girl?" He opened his right hand and I put my hand in his.

"I'm good, kinda salty, but I'm happy."

"Me too. So, how's it's going with your friend why didn't she come?"

"I don't know. I went to check on her the other day and she was gone, I called her phone a few times but it was just going straight to voicemail. I think she went back to her boyfriend, and that's so messed up. Kodi is a beautiful girl with such a fun personality. Even when she was all beat up she was still smiling and joking. Nobody deserves that."

"You did all you could Ki, the decision is ultimately up to her if she wanted to leave him alone. But, she could've just went back to where her family is."

"No, the way she talked, she would never go back home. I been praying for her though."

He kissed the back of my hand and we continued the drive home listening to music.

We got home, and I sat on the couch watching Deontae make 3 trips outside getting all of the gifts out the trunk. I don't even need to have a baby shower, I'll have a diaper party, I know newborns shit a lot, you can never have enough diapers.

"Man, we gone need a house if we keep getting stuff."

"We can put some stuff at my apartment, whatever we don't need right now."

"Why do you even still have that?"

"I don't know." I shrugged my shoulders, and start picking my nails. I think I just kept it as a just in case. People change every day, and the last thing I need is for Deontae to decide this isn't what he wants anymore; then me and my baby is homeless.

"Sublease it and move your stuff out, except the furniture. I'll buy us a house somewhere in the suburbs."

"Um, no that is too far for me to be driving every day for work." He face scrunched up and mine did too. "What's your problem?"

"I didn't know you was gone continue going to work." I laughed and I really didn't mean to, but I know he couldn't be serious right now.

"And what else would I do?"

"I mean I'm not saying just stay home with the baby, but I think you should take like a year off."

"Why can't you take a year off?"

He left out a little cocky laugh and changed his posture. "I can't just take a year off Kiarra, come on."

"Oh, so because I don't have a Dr. in front of my name my job isn't important?"

"You know that's not what I mean, don't make this bigger than what it is, you stressing my baby out."

"I'm going to bed. Do me a favor and don't come in there tonight, thanks, good night."

"Are you seriously mad right now? I'm too damn big for this couch Kiarra." I didn't respond as I grabbed his pillow out the room and threw it at him.

I closed the room door and locked, I'm glad I got a bathroom and some snacks in here because I don't plan on leaving out of here.

***

I woke up in the middle of the night to relieve my bladder, and got a craving for my *Chips Ahoy* I had in the cabinet. I opened the door slowly and heard Deontae snoring, so I walked out and went to the kitchen.

Deontae had the couched pulled together and was laid across both of them. I knew he was gone use that doctor brain and figure something out.

When I got to the kitchen, and I didn't see my cookies, my heart dropped. I stormed to the living room and tapped on Deontae's head.

"Deontae!" he jumped up and looked around with a concerned look on his face.

"What's wrong, the baby ok?"

"Where are my cookies?" he squinted his eyes at me, and looked at the time on the cable box.

"You serious right now, it's three in the morning?"

"I'm well aware of the time, what I can't get is why my cookies aren't where I left them. Did you eat my cookies Deontae?"

"Ki, go to bed it's too early for this."

I stormed to the light to turn it on, and went back to standing over him. "I'm not going anywhere until you answer my question."

He released a deep breath and sat up to look me in my eyes. "Yes, I ate your cookies baby, I'm sorry, do you want me to go get you some more?"

"I can't believe you would eat all of my cookies, you have all those other chips and healthy bullshit, and you eat MY cookies?!" I was now crying with snot coming out my nose and everything.

It was one thing you could do that'll really hurt me, and that's eat something of mine, and not even leave ME some. It was originally my shit anyway, he was at the grocery store with me, and said he didn't really care for them. I feel like he did this to spite me, for him sleeping on the couch. If I found out he did one of those damn how to eat Chips Ahoy videos I'm killing him.

"Come on baby girl calm down, I'm getting up... I'll go get some more, so lay back down, I'm sorry."

He jumped up to put his pants back on, and

grabbed a sweatshirt out the closet. I laid back down and waited for him to come back. When he did come back he had a *7-Eleven* bag in his hand and it was full of *Chips Ahoy, Oreos, Lorna Doone, and Keebler fudge stripe* cookies.

"And I'm sleeping in this bed, that couch uncomfortable as hell, I gotta be up in 3 hours."

"Ok." I lowkey needed him so I could go back to sleep, but I was letting him think he put his foot down.

I ate my cookies, as Deontae continued his snoring in the bed. I got on Facebook, and looked at all the pictures from the party I was tagged in. I can't wait to meet my daughter, I hope she's a little chocolate drop like her daddy.

FIFTHTEEN

Kodi

I've been in the hospital for 3 months while my body healed. The police came to the hospital asking if I'll testify against Gates, and I told his ass hell naw! I know he tried to kill me before, but he will definitely kill me if I even thought about talking to the police. I don't even know who called them, but I'm glad they did. I was finally being released, and I was glad one of my nurses had some gutta brothers who went to pack my stuff for me. I was going to be in a hotel for a while, but with all the money I took from Gates, I was going to find me a small studio somewhere. Kiarra's neighborhood is nice as hell, but I know it cost more than what I want to spend. I am glad that I finally got my phone, so I can try to reach out to her.

"You ready to go?" Gerald, my nurse's brother, agreed to take me to my hotel since I had all of my bags, and no car.

"Yeah, thanks again for this."

"It aint shit beautiful." I had to look up to make sure he was talking to me. I mean, I knew I use to be pretty but with these new scars, I'm not too sure.

They told me I had to ride in a wheelchair out, so I sat down while Gerald pushed me to his car that was parked at the door.

I got in and put my seatbelt on, as he walked around the back of the car to get to the driver's side.

"Where you gone be staying at?"

"Just take me to the *Hilton*, I might as well be comfortable while I find a place." He drove the short distance to the hotel, and helped me out the car when we got there.

I got me a room for a week, and Gerald brought my bags up to my room.

"If you need anything, don't hesitate to call me." He handed me a business card and wrote his number on the back.

"You're a producer?"

"Yeah, I do a little bit of this and that. I gotta head out though, don't forget to use that number, keep your head up."

"I will, thanks again." He left out and I got comfortable in the bed with my phone in my hand.

I had been debating with myself if I should call Kiarra or not. I really needed a friend to talk to, but I didn't want to be judged for my decisions. Throwing caution in the wind, I dialed her number and she answered on the second ring sounding half sleep.

"Hello?"

"Hey Kiarra."

"Kodi? Where the hell you been, are you ok?"

"No, but I will be. I been in the hospital." I heard her gasp loudly and then a bunch of moving around in

"What hospital are you at? Why didn't you call me before now it's been months?"

"I didn't have any of my things until recently. I'm going to be staying at the *Hilton,* I gotta find a place I can afford. If you're not busy, can you stop by?

"Yeah, I can come now, I was just laying around anyway, are you hungry? I'll grab something on the way."

"Yes, thank you, I'll text you my room number."

"Ok boo, see you soon."

I got cleaned up and washed my hair so I can get the smell of the hospital off of me. I didn't have any hair products, so I had to just wear my hair in the natural curly state.

An hour later, I heard knocks at the door, and Kiarra was standing there with a perfectly round stomach.

"Hi, you're getting so big, you're beautiful pregnant."

"Awww, thanks, I have 2 more months until my little girl get here."

She came in and sat on the couch, and put a *Popeyes* bag on the coffee table.

"I only eat wings I hope that's ok."

"That's fine."

"So, do you want to tell me what happened or is it still too sensitive?"

"Well, I got bored so I went back to the house. At first, he wasn't there, but when I was cooking dinner, he came in and had the nerve to have a woman with him. I started to snap on him, and he grabbed the pot of mashed potatoes off the stove and hit me with it. He burned me pretty bad, and I think the woman he brought in called the police because he was arrested, and I was rushed to *Christ* hospital. I was there up until today, and that's everything."

"OhmiGod, I'm so sorry you went through that. if you want to move in my place you can, I can have my personal stuff cleaned out by the end of the week, it's paid up for the next 2 years, you just take care of the utilities. I was so worried about you and I prayed for you every day."

"I don't know what to say, but thank you. you have been nothing but great since we met, and I really appreciate this."

"It's ok, but if you go back to him I swear I will stomp my pregnant ass over there with my gun and drag you out myself."

We shared a laugh as we ate our food.

"Trust me I'm not going anywhere near him. Besides, I think I met someone who seems like a pretty nice guy."

"Who? How you meet somebody when you was in the hospital?"

"Welllll, he's my nurse's brother, and he went with his two brothers to get all of my clothes and stuff from Gate's house."

"How did you meet him? I really hope he's not into the same shit yo last dub was into."

"No, he's a producer, and he's related to my nurse at the hospital. She said she wanted to help me, and she did."

"Ok, I think I need to interview him before I this goes any further."

"Yes ma'am."

We laughed, and talked for a few hours, before she left because she had to cook dinner for her boyfriend.

She always looked happy whenever she talked about her boyfriend, and I couldn't wait to find someone who made me smile from my soul.

****

The week I spent in the hotel, I pampered myself with massages, facials, and I stayed in the bed all day. I was set to move into Kiarra's apartment tomorrow, and I forgot I didn't have a way to get there with my stuff. I played with Gerald's card for a minute, and decided I would just text him instead of calling.

Me: *Hey this is Kodi, sorry if I'm disturbing you, but I was wondering if you could help me move into my place tomorrow.*

Gerald: *Wassup beautiful? I got you, I'm glad you finally decided to hit my line*

Me: *sorry I've been getting my head together*

Gerald: *it's cool, I understand that.*

Me: *are you busy?*

Gerald: *lil' bit, I'm in a session, I can give you call when I get out of here.*

Me: *ok I'll talk to you later*

I was smiling and couldn't wait until tomorrow came so I could see his sexy baby face. Gerald looked like he was 19, when he was really 27. He wore these glasses, but still squinted his eyes when he stared at me like he was trying to read my life through my eyes.

Instead of calling, Gerald popped up after midnight when he was done in the studio. we stayed up all night talking, and surprisingly it was easy to open to him. I told him about my toxic relationship with Gates, and how my family basically disowned me for moving away with him.

He opened up to me about his past, and how his father used to beat him, his mom, and siblings ass whenever he got bored. He said music is what stopped him from running the streets and doing dumb shit with his friends, who are all either in jail, or dead. It was cool how he could look back at shit he went through and joke about it... one day I hoped I could do the same.

***

After Gerald brought my last bag in the house, I took some meat out the freezer so I could make us a big lunch. Since he would let me pay him, he agreed to me cooking him something. I was going to tap into my inner Italian and make us some pork chops, spaghetti, and homemade meatballs. I was going to make a small salad to go on the side, and I'm sure I was going to be laid out sleep after I finish eating.

"This place nice as fuck, it's kinda far from me, but I'll make a trip for you."

"Aw you plan on seeing me some more?"

"Yeah is that a problem with you?"

"Not at all, I thought I would've ran you off with the stuff I told you last night."

"Nah baby, I aint weak, and the stuff you told me just shows that you been through a lot, but you didn't it break you. You're beautiful, and deserve to be treated like the Queen you are, that's why I was led to you. If you let me, I can show you how it feels to be with a real man." He licked his lips and I had to clamp my legs tight before I have Gerald bless my new crib.

"That sound good to me."

"Aite, I'll tell you now, I'm in the studio a lot, but you can come down there when I'm there, if I'm not with somebody."

"That's cool, you know I do a little singing, I'll slide in the booth too."

"Stop playing you know how to sing? Let me hear something hit a note or some shit."

"No, I'm shy, but I can sing."

"So how you gone get in the booth?"

"I could block it out in there. If you don't believe me just take me to the studio the next time you go."

"I got a session tomorrow with Banks, but you can come before he get there, show me what you got Miss Kodi.

I hopped out of my stool and hugged him around his neck. "You don't understand how excited I am, thank you for this."

It was always my dream to be famous singer, but when I met Gates, I chose to follow him state to state instead of pursuing my goals. Now it's finally time to focus on what makes me happy.

Beeep!

The sound of the microwave snapped me out of my thoughts, and I got the ground beef out to make my meatballs.

"So, you mixed or something?"

"Why you mean am I mixed?"

"I meeaann, you white as hell, and making meatballs... I'm tryna see if I need to be looking out for the mafia outside or something." I start laughing and Gerald joined in showing off that sexy ass smile. It was something about a man that had nice white teeth that just drove me crazy.

"Well for one, I'm not Italian; my father is black, and my mom is white."

"Aw ok, that's cool so you might know how to cook. Was yo pops around?"

"I mean yeah, when my mom let him be. They broke up when I was about 9 and my mom hated him for moving on. You know how that goes with bitter women... I think I saw my every other month. He snuck and bought me a phone, and my mama beat my ass when she caught me talking to him." I laughed and put my meatballs in the oven.

"That's crazy as hell, that's why I'm glad I aint got no kids yet. No disrespect, but bitches be using they babies as pawns, when they the ones suffering. I'll kill a bitch over my seed, and not think twice about it."

"Woah, that's a bit extreme don't ya think?"

"Nope."

He kept his answer short and simple, and I just shook my head and got my pork chops seasoned and battered for me to fry.

Gerald stayed in the kitchen the entire time I cooked, and made beats on the table.

"You was one of them irritating kids that beat on

tables and did the *Grinding* beat with pens, weren't you?"

"Hell yeah, niggas aint wanna battle me at lunch."

"You so silly, wash your hands, so you can eat."

I made our plates as he washed his hands in the kitchen sick.

"What you want to drink?"

"Some water." I grabbed him a bottle of water, and I grabbed a pineapple crush before I joined him at the table.

"This shit smell good as hell, I hope I don't die from food poison or something."

"Don't try to treat me Gerald, I can cook!"

He bowed his head and head my hands so he could bless our food.

"Thank you, Father, for this meal, I hope it's not my last meal, but I'm putting my trust into Kodi, so she could do the same for me. Amen."

"Amen."

I smiled and dug into my food, I'm so happy that I met Gerald, even if it is at one of the lowest points of my life.

SIXTEEN

Lauren

Banks had been dragging me around with him whenever I wasn't working, trying to prove himself to me I guess.

We walked into his studio and the producer was playing back a record with a female singing. The shit sounded dope as fuck and Banks was nodding his head to it too.

"Damn who is that?" I asked sitting down next to the female that was in here. For her sake, I hope she came in here for Gerald.

"My girl Kodi over here, she got vocal bruh, you tryna hop on this track?"

"Hell yeah, run it back." Gerald started the song over, and I turned facing Kodi with my legs crossed.

"So you supposed to be Kiarra's new friend huh?"

"Yeah, we're pretty close. How are you doing I heard a lot about you?" I don't like new friends, but if she was cool with Ki, then I was going to TRY to be nice.

"I am blessed thank you. And I want to thank you for helping my best friend out."

"She helped me too, so you don't have to thank me."

Kodi stayed and recorded 3 more songs with Banks, and some alone. Gerald was staring at her like she was a juicy ass steak and I had to hand him some water to cool his ass down.

****

After the session was done, we had to rush to his house to pack a bag, because he had to go to Atlanta for a show.

We only had an hour to get changed before he bad to be at the *Philips Arena* for the show.

There was a bunch of new artist, and some old. I know I was excited to see Migos, with they non talking asses.

"Lo just chill right here, next to the stage, don't try to go in the crowd; yo little ass gone get trampled out there."

"Fuck you. have a good show though baby."

Banks hit the stage and the crowd went crazy. I got my camera from my bookbag and start snapping shots of him and the crowd.

He came back sweaty as hell, and breathing hard.

"You killed that shit bae!"

"Wassup Banks, how long you gon' be in the A?"

"I'm out here wassup?"

"Slide to the studio later, I know we can put together a hit bro."

"Good looking, just send me the information."

I stood to the side star struck staring at Takeoff.

"Hellloooo, I'm Lauren I'm here for all of your photography needs, here's my card, I travel just send me a location and I'm there. Go on my website to check out some samples, all of my social media is on the card as well, shout a sister out, good show."

I stepped in before they left and gave myself a quick plug... aint no shame in my game. Banks laughed at me and we went to his designated dressing room.

"Thank you for sticking by me baby, I appreciate you for real."

"No problem baby you know I got you like you got me."

We watched the show from the back, and followed everyone to the club where *Migos* was hosting an after party.

We turnt up at *MJQ Concourse* for a few hours and ended up at *Magic City* until they closed at 3 in the morning.

"I'm sleepy as hell, but I need something to eat." I slurred, as Banks was driving us to our hotel. I was drunk as hell in the passenger seat and needed something to eat before I threw up everywhere.

"Aite baby, it's something by the hotel."

We pulled up to *Metro Café Diner* and he parked by the door.

"What they make here bae?"

"Lo... I never been here either, I can't tell you that."

"All you had to say was I don't know." We got out the car and walked into the diner. Anything gone be good right about now.

The entire time we were in the diner, Banks was on his phone, and I was ready to smash it on the table.

"What's so good in your phone that I can't even get small talk from you?"

"Huh?"

"If you can huh, you can hear."

"Stop tweaking, you done eating and shit."

"Naw. I'm bout to order some more shit."

"Lo, I'm just taking care of business, don't be like that."

I ignored him and finished my burger and fries I ordered. When I was done, Banks paid and we went to the hotel to get some sleep before he had to be back up to be in the studio.

I'm sitting out on the next trip; this shit is messing up my sleep.

SEVENTEEN

Kiarra

I had a month before Halloween, and that's the same day my baby girl was supposed to come into the world, and I couldn't wait until this pregnancy was over. I was still working, and my feet usually look like fluffy pillows by the end of my shift. Deontae had been begging me to go on maternity leave, so I put my two weeks in, and today is my last day.

Kim out together a mini, last day party at the Nurse's station, and she had cupcakes and everything. Some people brought my baby girl some gifts, like she needed anything else.

We still hadn't decided on a name so for now she was the new 'Baby girl'.

"I'm going to miss you boo, but I'll try to take some vacation days if you need a hand, just let me know."

"Thanks boo, but with her dad and grandparents, I know I'll be covered."

"What time are you off?"

"Now, I was trying to wait for Deontae but I see he's going to be in there for a while."

"I'll let him know you left so he won't look for you. Text me later boo."

"Ok, see you later."

I grabbed the few gifts I had and took the elevator to the parking garage. When I got in my car, I took my shoes off and I felt so much relief through my body.

"Can you hear me out Kiarra?"

"Aaahh!! What the hell Church, why are you in my backseat?" I grabbed my gun and pointed it at his head, and he threw his hands up in surrender.

"I was waiting for the perfect time to talk to you. You look beautiful pregnant, I wish it was my baby, but I know you'll never forgive me."

"Get the fuck out my car! I listened to your I'm sorry speech over dinner, and you was bussing me upside my damn head a couple months later."

"I was in a fucked up space, popping pills, and I wasn't thinking straight. I know you're the reason I'm still breathing, and I want to say thank you for that."

"I didn't do it for you trust me, you go home and thank Mia and your new baby. Now get out of my car before I forget I'm in the forgiving mood." With that being said he kept his hands up and got out the back seat. I locked the doors, and hit the button to start my car. When I turned the radio on and heard Kodi's single *Money Signs* on 107.5 I was singing along and dancing in my seat as I drove home. Gerald seemed to be good for her; she had been so happy lately, and her arm and chest was healing so nicely. I just hate that she had to be in that situation at all.

I made it home, and looked through take out menus, because I was not cooking tonight. I decided on jerk, and I know I was going to hear Tae's mouth, but it was his daughter that had me craving it.

***

Bzzz

I woke up on the couch, with my phone ringing in my hand.

"Hello?"

"You was sleep baby?"

"Yeah, but I'm up now. Are you done for the day?"

"I just finished up, so I'm about to head out in a minute. Do you want me to pick up dinner?"

"Yeah, I wanted some jerk, but I changed my mind, and I want some *Aloha Eats*." That was a Hawaiian restaurant that was down the street, and their food was always on point.

"I'm glad you change yo mind about the jerk because I would've had to shut that down baby. What you want me to get you tho?"

"I want some BBQ chicken saimin, grilled salad, a side of macaroni salad, and a strawberry guava juice."

"That's weird as hell Kiarra, but I'll see you in a minute Queen."

"Ok, love you."

I went to the baby's room and moved stuff around for the hundredth time. Deontae walked in when I was moving the changing table, and he looked like he wanted to curse me out.

"What I tell you about moving this stuff man, come eat."

"Gimme kiss Tae, don't be mad, it's not even heavy."

The look on his face said, 'yeah whatever', but he

gave me a kiss anyway, and sat the food on the bed.

"You nesting, that's why you been doing all this, baby girl about to make her entrance."

"Imma need you to stop listening to yo mama Deontae, I am not nesting I still have 4 and a ½ weeks left."

"What are we gone name her bae, I'm tired of just saying baby girl?"

I sat Indiana style and opened my food up, while he stripped out of his clothes and got ready for a shower.

"I don't know, have you been thinking of names?"

"I'll think while I'm in the shower."

He went into the bathroom, and I ate my food, while I was watching *Love and Hip Hop*, I don't even know what I'm watching anymore with these fools.

"How about Kenzie" Deontae came out the bathroom dripping with water, and his towel wrapped around his waist, but it did nothing to hide the monster underneath it. I don't know why but my sex drive has been so high lately, it seemed like I was always horny.

"What you say?"

"If you stop raping me with yo eyes, you can hear me talking to you. I said how about Kenzie, for baby girl's name?"

"I like that, and her middle name can be Denise, I always liked that name."

"Kenzie Denise Blak... I like that, I can't wait to see her and hold her man."

"You wanna have her at home, then we can tell the world how you delivered her yourself?" Deontae's face was twisted up in disgust and I couldn't help but to laugh.

"It was a joke, I don't want you anywhere down there, you will never look at me the same."

"Trust me, I'm staying at the head of the bed."

He put his boxers on and climbed in the bed. "Everybody's last name is going to be Blak except yours, when you wanna change that?"

I choked on my food, and had to take a drink to wash it down.

"You ok?"

"Yeah, I was eating too fast."

"Ok, so answer the question."

"I mean, I don't know, whenever you want to propose, I'm already stuck with you for life." I laughed and he playfully pushed me.

"Ok, I got you."

He ate his food then rubbed my feet until I fell asleep. I can honestly say I'm lucky to have Deontae in my life.

EIGHTEEN

Kodi

I loved the fall time, because all the pumpkin flavored stuff were brought back. I was in the studio recording with Gerald, but I need a break, so I walked to *Dunkin Donuts* and got me a pumpkin spice latte. My phone rang when I was walking back, so I stood outside and answered it.

"Hello?"

There wasn't anyone on the phone, but it was a recording stating the Gates was being released from jail. My stomach was in knots as I walked back in the studio.

"Damn took you long enough, I thought you got lost. What's wrong Kodi"

"Gates is being released from jail, what if he comes looking for me what am I supposed to do?"

"Relax baby. I got you, imma protect you no matter what."

He hugged me tight and I inhaled the intoxicating scent of his Tom Ford *Oud Wood for Men*.

"Let's get back to work, if you want to hire a security team, then I'll get on that right away, you know my brothers live for shit like this."

"It's ok, maybe I'll just go to the gun range and learn to shoot. Hopefully it never comes down to that."

"If anything happens, you make sure you call me asap, aite?"

"I got it, thank you. I'm ready to finish now."

I went into the booth and poured my heart out on the record. It was therapy for me to be able to sing my pain away.

I stayed in the studio until I had to leave for his next appointment to come in. He had one of his brothers come drive me home, and I was grateful because I probably would've had a heart attack if I had to go alone, especially after that call I got earlier.

My new place was like a peace pad, when I walked in the door, all my worries were left on the other side of the door.

Gerald: *Wanna do something tonight?*

Me: *like what?*

Gerald: *just be ready at 9*

This was definitely something I could get used to. Gerald always popped up on me with something for us to do, and he haven't even tried to have sex with me. Now, he did let me know that he'll tear it up whenever I wanted him to.

While I was waiting for the tub to fill up, I called to check on Kiarra. She still had 2 weeks to go, and she was so miserable. Her diaper party was last week, and all she kept saying was she couldn't wait to have little miss Kenzie.

"Hey boo, wassup?"

"Nothing I was just checking on you."

"I'm good girl, laying down as always, I'm just so tiiiiirreeedd! And this little girl is taking forever to come. I been walking with Tae in the morning, and it aint doing nothing, she already head down and everything."

"She sound like a stubborn little Scorpio."

"Leave my baby alone, what you up to?"

"About to take a bath, and get ready to go out with Gerald."

"Y'all are so cute, well you go have fun, and text me later, I need to get a few more minutes of rest before I have to finish cooking."

"Ok, take it easy, and call me if the baby come tonight."

I got in tub and soaked for 30 minutes until I got out to get dressed. It was kinda chilly out, but I wanted to be cute, so I put on a gray long sleeve sweater dress, and black thigh high boots. I had just got my hair done at *The Shop* and Lovely had hooked my hair up as usual, so all I had to do was take my bonnet off and shake my curls free. I beat my face, and was putting my wallet in my purse when there was a knock at the door.

"Damn, you look good as hell, you ready?"

"Yeah, let's go." We walked out the door and I locked up the apartment.

"Where are we going?"

"Out to eat first, then I'm going to take you to my spot I go when I want to clear my head."

We pulled up to s spot called *Eddie V's Prime Seafood,* and I could smell the food all the way outside. We walked in and was led right to our table, that was in the corner of the restaurant.

"You want some wine or some shit?"

"No, I want to try one of these 24 Karat Cocktails, it sound good."

We ordered our drinks and made small talk while we looked over the menu. "So how are you feeling Kodi, with the music and shit?"

"I like it, and we work great together." I heard a familiar loud laugh, and the hairs on the back of my neck stood up. I peeked over and saw Gates sitting at a table with a female.

"You ok Kodi?"

"Huh? Yeah, I'm ok, you ready to order?" I was still looking at the table, and Gerald followed my eyes.

"You know them or something?"

"That's him." I whispered like he was going to hear me over the loud chatter in the restaurant.

"Your ex?"

"Yeah."

He nodded his head, and pulled his phone out.

"What are you doing?"

"Nothing."

NINETEEN

Gerald

"Gerald please don't do nothing."

"I aint doing nothing, do you want to leave?"

"You planned this evening out, I don't wanna mess anything up."

"I want you to enjoy yourself, and I know you won't be able to do that here, food don't look that good anyway, come on." She drunk the last of her drink and I threw a hundred dollar bill on the table to cover our drinks,

"What you got a taste for?"

"I don't know, this is your city, what would you recommend?"

"If you aint too bougie, I can take you to a spot that never closes."

"Trust me I'm not bougie, I was about to eat me some gourmet noodles until you said something." We were riding and the lights from the city was shining down on her, and her skin looked to be glowing.

I pulled into *Maxwell Street Polish* and the smell of onions was thick in the air.

"Ooohh I haven't had a good polish in a long time, we gone have to grab some gum because I want extra grilled onions on mine." She got out the car smiling like it was the best place in the world. This was one thing I really like about Kodi… it didn't take much to satisfy her, but I would do anything I could to keep her happy.

I ordered us 2 polishes with everything on it, and she sat on the trunk of my Dodge Charger, while I stood between her legs.

"I really like the feeling I get when I'm with you."

"Aw yeah?"

"Yea Gerald, I feel so alive, like nothing could bring me down from this high."

Our order was called and when I walked off to get it I heard tires screeching and gunshots.

SKKKEERRRRRT! POW! POW! POW!

"Aaahhh!" I ran back to my car as the car sped off and saw Kodi laying on the ground with a splatter of blood on my back window.

"Shit! Where you hit at baby?"

"Aaarrrrgggghh, I don't know, are you ok?"

"I'm fine, come on let me help you up." There was blood all over the top of her dress where I saw a small hole.

"I can't go to a hospital, he's going to kill me, he's not going to stop until he kills me." She broke down crying and it was pulling at my heart strings to see her hurting like this over that dub ass nigga she was with.

"Look at me Kodi, I promise I won't let nothing happen to you as long as I got breath in my body."

We got in the car and I sped to Deontae's house that was closer than the hospital anyway. Me, Tae, and Banks, all grew up together and went to Morgan Park High School together.

Knock, knock!

"Whose house is this Gerald?"

"Just relax." I was holding her bridal style and waiting for somebody to come to the door. Deontae came to the door looking half sleep.

"Bro I need you and Kiarra's help."

He saw the blood on me and Kodi and woke up quick. He let us in and locked the door behind us. "Ki! Baby get up I need you in here."

"With what— Ohmigod what happened?" Kiarra ran back to their room and came back with a bunch of towels, and a big leather bag. Deontae grabbed a small let out bed from the closet and I was looking at these two sideways.

"Y'all used to doing this type of shit? Let me find out."

"She is." Deontae was in his pajamas but it was looking like a hospital room in their living room. "Lay her down and Ki grab a sheet to cover her up. I'm guessing you don't want this dress anymore do you?"

"Naw, I can order a new one." Kodi laughed and started to doze off from the medicine Kiarra gave her.

***

"Aite she's all stitched up, and she might be sleep for a few hours, you wanna stay here til morning?"

"Naahhh, I appreciate this bro, we just gone go to her place, since it's down the street. And I'll send someone to come clean this mess up."

"You good, just be careful out here."

I carried Kodi back to the car and drove the short

distance to her place. Ki had washed her up, so I laid her in the bed, and took her house keys when I left. I had plans to come back, but I had to take care of some shit first. Looking at all the blood I had all over me and my seat, had me seeing red.

"Yo?"

"Did you get anywhere with what I sent you?"

"I'm staring up at the stars right now, it's so sweet out here." My brother said speaking in code.

"Bet, send me yo location, I need to see it for myself."

"Say less."

When we left the restaurant earlier, I sent that nigga Gates picture to my brothers, and they was watching him for me since Kodi got shot.

I pulled up to a house on Paulina, and the block was dead. Perfect for me.

"So, we bout to light this bitch up?" I dapped my brothers Jerome and Darius up and hit the blunt Jerome was smoking.

"Naw, that's the easy way out, I'm going to the side door, Rome you go around back, and Darius watch the front door."

I was the oldest, so they followed my lead with no problem. This dumb nigga had his door unlocked like he was untouchable, and I was about to show him he wasn't. I pulled the gun from my back and screwed my silencer out before I walked in the house. The same shorty he was with in the restaurant was in the kitchen, so I sent one in to the back of her head and finished my stroll through the house. In my eyes, she was guilty too.

"Damn Imani what's taking so long?"

Wham!

I crashed my gun into his head and he fell to the floor.

"Dammnn! That nigga hit the floor hard as hell. Did you kill his ass already?"

"Drag this bitch outside, he aint dead yet." I grabbed a bucket, filled it with water and grabbed a bag of ice from his freezer. I walked out where they had Gates laid out on the pavement, and dumped the ice and water over his head, and he jumped up flopping like a fish out of water.

"Who the fuck is y'all?"

"You don't remember me nigga, you shot at me and my girl earlier."

"So, yo soft ass had to come with back up? Fuck outta here."

"Get yo bitch ass up."

The second he stood straight up I sent a blow to his face and he stumbled down the driveway. "Yo hoe ass aint tough without that gun huh?"

I continued to hit him, until he was laid out on the ground barely breathing. Jerome came and stomped his head to curb, and Darius sent a bullet through in chest.

"We'll get this cleaned up, leave yo clothes bro."

"Nigga I aint got no clothes to change into."

"That's why you need to stay in the studio, rookie. Go to our trunk and grab sumn, and put yours in the black bag... shoes too." I did what he said and drove home to grab some clothes to take back to Kodi's house. She was still sleep when I came in, and I went to the bathroom to shower and scrub every inch of my body.

When I got out, Kodi was groaning and trying to sit up in the bed.

"How you feeling?"

"I'm ok, a little groggy, where were you a little while ago?"

"I went home to grab some clothes, imma stay here and take care of you for a few days aite?"

"What about working?"

"I'll reschedule, I'm only working with Banks right now, and you. Don't worry about nothing, I got you."

She laid back down and we fell asleep while I was holding her from behind.

TWENTY

Deontae

We were at our last appointment for the baby, and Kenzie's due date was slowly approaching.

"Everything looks good with mommy and baby, you're only dilating 2 cm, but people can go weeks with no change. You can go for walks, when it's not too cold."

"Can I walk on a treadmill?"

"I don't recommend that, may not be the safest thing to do."

"Thanks Rob, she won't be on any of that." I helped Ki off the table and we went back home.

I used my vacation days, and had a month off to stay home and help with my baby girl. Ki walked around like it was the end of world because she was still pregnant. Right now she was walking up and down the hallway.

"Stop pacing and come relax baby girl."

"He said I need to walk Tae, don't you want to meet your stubborn daughter?" She sat next to me and I rubbed her feet.

"Mmmm, that feels so good you just don't understand."

"I can tell by all them noises you making. It don't even sound like that when I'm beating it up."

"Shut up Deontae, the way I feel, you'll never 'beat it up' again." She mocked me making a face and I stop rubbing her feet.

"Come ooonnn, why you stop?"

"What you say na? I don't think I heard you correctly."

"I'm just playing baby, you can beat it up now if that's gone help me have this baby."

"Naw, you aint about to use me."

"Fine, can you go get me a jerk salmon salad and one of those ginger beers for the heartburn I know I'm going to get?"

"You shouldn't even be eating that hot stuff, but I'll go get it."

I left out and had to take a 20 minute drive to *Uncle Joe's* in Hyde Park, because she said they were the only restaurant that made the food right.

****

"Deandra you better wait for me before you run off."

I heard a voice I haven't heard in a few years and I looked to see Starr, my ex and little girl walking to the restaurant.

"Starr?"

"Hey Deontae, how's it going? I haven't seen you in a long time."

"Yeah, I know, I've been good. How are you, and who's this?"

"This is, um... my daughter Deandra." This little girl looked to be about 6 or 7, and was a mirroring image of Starr.

"Before you ask, no, this is not your daughter."

"How old is she?"

"Just made 6, look, I'm sorry, college was a new experience for me, and I got a little crazy."

"So, you was sleeping around?"

Kiarra: *Baaaeee hurry we're starving!*

A text from Kiarra stopped me from snapping, and I just got in my truck and pulled off.

I walked in the house, and Ki was waiting at the kitchen table.

"What's wrong Tae?"

"Nothing, I'm ok."

"You sure?" Those hazel eyes I fell in love with was full of concern as she stared at me and ate her food at the same time.

"I'm positive baby, don't worry about me."

We ate and talked about football until Ki fell asleep on the couch.

I sat back thinking about everything, and I don't know why, but I was mad that Starr admitted to cheating… well I'm mad I never knew she was cheating. Then, to fake kill a baby that was never mine to begin with is just shady as hell.

Shit like that is the reason why I'm grateful for Kiarra. She was a little rough around the edges, but I know I never got to worry if she's being loyal or not.

*****

"Bae, I look like a whale, I'm not taking any pictures like this." Lauren scheduled us for a maternity shoot, and Kiarra was trying to change her outfit... AGAIN.

"You look fine bae." She was wearing Emerald colored an off the shoulder maxi dress, and she looked perfect to me.

Kiarra pouted and we left out to go to Lo's studio. When we got there Kiarra had another melt down because she thought she looked fat. Lauren did her "best friend" pep talk, and we was able to finish the shoot.

"Give me a few days, and I'll have these back for y'all. Bestie, go eat something because you're crazy; I can't wait to my Gbaby get here.

"Shut up Lauren."

We left, and Kiarra had me take her to *Giordano's* because she swore up down the baby had been craving it. My poor baby was a drama queen, but I had to get used to it because I plan on being with her for the rest of my life.

TWENTY ONE

Kiarra

It was the day before my due date, and still no baby. I was starting to feel like I was going to be pregnant forever. I had been doing everything to try to get this baby to come, and she's just being stubborn.

Banks had a show tonight, and I talked Deontae into going. But, looking at what he chose to wear, I was changing my mind.

"I don't think I like them pants bae." He let out his deep laugh because he followed my eyes and already knew what I was talking about.

"Come on Ki, you want me to stay home with you?"

"Nooo, go show your support, you never get out the house."

"Alright baby love you."

"Love you too."

He left out the door and I instantly got bored, and I knew I had nobody to talk to because everybody was going to the concert.

I got comfortable on the couch and turned on Hallmark. This is my favorite channel this time of year when they have their Countdown to Christmas.

An hour into my movie my phone was going on nonstop, and I thought something at the concert but it was a bunch of texts from an unknown number.

I'm so sorry Kiarra..

I miss my friend...

can we please talk

After the third text, I figured it was Church, so I put my phone down and resume watching my movie until he started to Facetime me. I hit accept and Church's sad face was in the camera.

"How did you get my number?"

"I always had it, I have my ways."

"What do you want, where is Miranda?"

"We not together… she knows I still love you, and she left me too."

"That sounds personal Church, I hope you don't think that's supposed to make me take you back?"

"You act like what we had wasn't shit Ki, how can you just walk away after we been tight for almost 4 years? Has that doctor nigga always been in the picture? You moved on fast as fuck ma."

"His name is Deontae, and unlike you, I'm faithful, so you can get the fuck off my phone saying dumb shit."

"Please don't hang up! I really need help; can we at least be friends?"

"Hell no! Did you forget the shit to did to me a few months ago? I didn't forget, and neither did my family, so I advise you to just stop popping up and calling me."

"I don't have anyone Ki, I been popping pills to ease the pain, but the shit aint working no more."

"Where's Tre?"

"He in his own shit, you really hate me that much I can't even talk to you?" He took a drink from a bottle of Hennessey, and I could tell he was drunk.

"Where are you?"

"Home."

"Send me your address, the second you try some shit, I'm shooting you where you stand, understood?"

"Thank you."

Whatever."

I hung up and threw on a black Nike track suit, and my Uggs, and left out the house. Church sent me his address, and I was praying I wasn't making a mistake by coming here. As stupid as it sounds, I do still have love for Church… now I would never be with him again, but I wouldn't want anything to happen to him.

When I pulled up to the address that was on 81st and Pulaski, I checked to make sure I had my knife, mace, and gun in my Birkin bag before I got out the car.

Church was standing on his porch waiting for me, and he tried to hug me when I got close to him.

"Un un Church, we not there at all."

"I'm sorry, I just didn't think you would actually come, you look good."

He was slurring and could barely walk, and I looked around at all the empty bottles he had laid around.

"You been drinking and popping pills Marshall, are you fucking stupid? Yo ass need rehab or something? Because that would be selfish if you did that to yo kids."

"No, I don't need no fucking rehab, I need you Ki. Can't you see how bad I'm doing without you? I need you, y-you make me better, make me want to do better."

I start feeling pain in my stomach, and I put my

hand on my stomach until it went away.

"You ok?"

"I'm fine, it was a mistake coming here, take care of yourself."

I heard a door slam, and Miranda came walking in the house with Mia, and a little boy who looked just like Church.

"Really? After you just begged us to come back, is this bitch pregnant with yo child Marshall?"

"Watch your mouth when you addressing me."

"Who the fuck are you supposed to be?"

"You know exactly who I am, but imma go before I have to drag you in front of your kids, pregnant and all bitch. Church... the next time you're feeling suicidal don't call me."

I walked out after I gave Mia a hug, and I heard Miranda snapping on him.

"Ki! Wait! I'm confused."

"You shouldn't be, I don't want yo ass! Ooowwww!" A sharp pain ripped through my body and I felt water trickling down my leg. "Are you freaking serious Kenzie?"

"Yo what the fu-- did yo water just break? Let me help you." Church reached for me again, and I smacked his hand away.

"Get yo ass in the house, you can't help me with nothing."

I got in the car and pulled off quickly. The contraction I was feeling wasn't close together so I raced home, and called Deontae.

"Hey bae you ok?" His background was loud, and he answered the phone screaming.

"Stop yelling Tae, it's time!"

"I can't hear you Ki."

I hung up and texted him instead because he was getting on my nerves being so loud.

Me: *Your baby is coming!*

He called me right back and I heard was a bunch of rustling noise and him cursing in the background.

"I'm on my way baby, I shouldn't have left you, shit."

"It's ok just hurry."

"Hold my baby in there until I get home, call your mom, I know she's closer than me."

"Ok."

I hung up and walked as fast as I could inside so I could change out of the wet clothes. The contractions were now 4 minutes apart so I called my mom and prayed she was still up.

"Hey Chubbz, why you still up?"

"The baby is coming, and Deontae isn't here, please come get me and take me to the hospital."

"Shit Kiarra, I was just about to go get me some food, I'm about 10 minutes away, but I'll be there in 5."

I grabbed my hospital bag, and got on the elevator. By the time I made it outside, my mom's car was pulling up and she hopped out the passenger side before the car even stopped.

"How far are the contractions? Are you in pain? Did

you call your doctor to let him know?"

"Ma, relax. Hi Vince, get your woman."

We made it to the hospital in record time, and I was wheeled up to my private room right away. I texted everyone that it was finally time as I was getting my vitals done, and I was praying Deontae made it in time.

My mom was in the room with me while Vince sat in the waiting room. After 20 minutes my cervix was checked and I was 7 cm dilated.

"Looks like it's almost baby time! Where's Dr. Blak?"

"I'm here, I'm here, did I miss it, are you ok?"

"Right on time, it should be any minute now the way she's progressing."

Deontae came to the head of the bed and kissed me. "Sorry I'm late."

"It's ok, you're here now."

"Deontae, you so petty! You saw me running to the elevators, tried to make me miss my God baby's arrival. Hey boo, how you feeling?"

Lauren came stomping in the room and gave Deontae a dirty look.

"My bad Lo, yo lil' legs was moving too slow, baby girl would've been here if I waited on you."

"Aite Jolly green giant, you got jokes today, don't let the first thing yo daughter see is me knocking you out."

I was laughing at them until a contraction hit and shut me right up.

"Aaahhh! Please get your baby out of me Deontae!"

"Nah, I told you I can't go down there, I'll get help though." He strolled out the room and I wanted to throw something at him.

"Stop pushing Ki, just wait for them to come check you." My mom was looking at monitors next to my bed, and acting like she was my nurse.

"I can't-- aahhh help it! Ma can you just deliver her, you're a nurse you know what you doing, I trust you mommy!"

"I'm off duty boo, sorry."

Deontae came rushing back in with a doctor, and stood back at the head of the bed.

"You are such a punk." Lauren said laughing at how scary Deontae was acting.

"Ok, you're fully dilated, I want you to take a deep breath in and push through your next contraction."

I did what he said, and all I heard was everyone yelling for me to keep going.

"Ok, that was good Kiarra. Get her oxygen, and we're going to do it again."

"Ok, I'm ready. I'm ready." I was talking more to myself than anyone else, as I took another deep breath and pushed as hard as I could.

"Keep going Ki, it'll be over soon, I promise, just keep pushing." Deontae was wiping my forehead with a cold towel and coaching me as I pushed again.

"Ohmigod Ki! I see her head, look Ki she coming!"

"How am I going to look Lauren? Aahhhh!"

The next sound I heard was my baby girl screaming at the top of her lungs, and it was music to my ears.

"Congratulations, your baby girl looks beautiful."

Deontae cut the umbilical cord, and let the nurse clean Kenzie up as I delivered the placenta and got cleaned up.

"You did good Ki, I'm so proud of you, Miss Kenzie is so beautiful." My mom was crying as she hugged me, and it made me cry too.

"Thank you mommy, I'm so happy you're here to witness this."

I looked over a Deontae and he was just staring down at Kenzie as they cleaned her up and put a diaper on her. I'm mad everybody else got a look at my baby before me and I'm the one who had to carry for 5 years.

"I know that look, I'll let you be the first to hold her Kiarra." the nurse handed me my daughter and I was in love. She didn't really have any color yet, but her ears were dark; so, I hope she be a chocolate drop like her daddy. Kenzie had my eyes, but she looked exactly like Deontae, down to his lips.

Deontae parents came in, and his mother was crying already. "Hey, Kiarra, you look great, let me see my grandba—aawww she is so cute, and she got those dangerous eyes like her mama, Deontae you gon' be in trouble son."

"Ma, that's not funny."

"I'm not joking hell."

My mom reached for Kenzie, and she took a million pictures of her before Deontae's mom held her next.

Lauren was standing in the corner mad because I'm sure she wanted to hold her too. I gave her a look and she huffed before she sat back and folded her arms across her chest.

"I'm so happy to have my first grandbaby, and it's a girl, I'm going to steal you all the time."

"Oh, no, my granddaughter gon' be with her Nana, aint that right?"

"Ok, for one both of you are wrong, my baby will be at home with her mother and father."

Kodi and Gerald showed up later in the day, and Kodi just kept saying how she had baby fever. She even bought my baby her first costume, and she was a pumpkin. So far all she did was sleep and that was ok with me.

Everybody left when I started falling asleep in the middle of talking, and Deontae stayed up standing over Kenzie's bed while she slept. My poor baby was going to be in trouble, her daddy wasn't letting her out of his sight.

TWENTY TWO

Deontae

Today was the day, Kenzie and Kiarra was finally coming home, and I was nervous as hell driving with her in the car. Kiarra kept complaining that I was driving too slow the whole ride to the house. I kept on driving passed the exit to the apartment building, and Kiarra smacked her lips.

"Where are we going baby, I'm ready to lay down?"

"We're going home."

"No, we just passed the exit, so what's going on?"

"You said you wanted a push present right?"

"No, you didn't. Deontae did you buy a house?"

"Not a house… I bought a condo, and we got way more room bae, I know you'll like it."

She just smiled in the backseat while I drove to our new home on Michigan Ave. There was a doorman, and he opened the back door for Kiarra to get out. It had just started to snow, and Kiarra had Kenzie covered up as we went inside. We took the elevator to the top floor, and Kiarra's eyes were big as she walked inside.

"This place is big as hell Tae; how much was it?"

"Don't worry about all that, it's paid for baby."

Kenzie was sleep, so we put her in her crib, and turned the baby monitor on.

"We have a baby… I can't believe this, she's finally here, and I have my body back."

"How long before we can start on my Junior."

"Deontae, please leave them drugs alone baby."

We laughed and Kiarra laid down to take a nap while Kenzie's sleep. I love my little family and couldn't wait to marry the love of my life.

****

It's Kiarra's birthday weekend, but I know she doesn't want to do anything outside of the house since Kenzie is only 2 weeks old. I was planning on proposing on her birthday which was tomorrow, and I had it set up to have a big dinner at the house. I hired a chef, and I hope everything turns out how I wanted.

"Damn cuddy, I can't believe you about to get married man, I'm proud of you son."

"Maaann shut up, I'm proud of you for sticking with one woman all this time."

"I aint have no choice, Lauren crazy as hell she'll fuck around and kill my ass; aint no other bitch worth my life, feel me?"

I just shook my head and waited for the jeweler to come back with the ring I had customized for Kiarra.

"Yo, aint that Church bitch ass over there?" I turned my head and instantly saw red. Since my daughter and girl was healthy, I had let any thoughts of revenge go… but, seeing this nigga just out spending money and living life, like he didn't violate was pissing me off.

"Yeah, that's him."

"What you wanna do bro, you know I stay ready?"

"It's cool, I gotta get home to my family, I can't get in no trouble." As soon as the word left my mouth, Church approached us. I saw Banks reaching behind him, and I just pray his crazy ass don't shoot him in this store.

"I aint come over here on no bullshit, I just want to come to you as a man and apologize for everything. I talked to Ki, and I know she aint gone ever forgive me, but let her know I meant everything I said."

"This nigga serious right now?" Banks was laughing and I was counting down from 100 in my head because I was ready to knock this nigga out.

"Bro you need to gone head about yo day before I forget I got a career to hold on to. And stay away from my girl, it aint no threat, it's a warning… and I mean everything I say too."

"You got that." he nodded his head and walked out the store, and I grabbed my phone to text Kiarra.

Me: *you got something you want to tell me?*

Ki: *no like what?*

Me: *we'll talk when I get home*

Ki: *you ok?*

"Here you are sir, all wrapped up and ready, good luck." Before I could respond the jeweler came out with the ring.

"Thanks." I grabbed the box and stuffed it in my pocket, and walked out the store.

"Don't do nothing crazy when you get home bro, just hear her out before you react."

"Fuck is there to hear out? She still been talking to

this nigga, I'm starting to think she set that shit up to run away with his ass or something."

"You sound dumb as fuck G; Ki was messed up… now unless she just like that freaky wild punch me shit, then I can't see that happening. She a real one, I don't think she on no snake shit bro. Now, if it was that Starr bitch, whatever they saying she did, she did that shit, she guilty as fuck." He was mocking 50 cent in *Power* and I had to laugh at this clown.

"Man I ran into her ass a few weeks ago, she had a little girl with her. You know she told me she was cheating on my ass?"

"I aint surprised, bitch use to look at me like she wanted to swallow my mans every time I saw her. I told you front jump don't trust her ass. So, how much did Ki snap when you told her bout that shit?"

"I aint tell her, it wasn't shit to tell really."

"But you over there about to rip the steering wheel off 'cuz she aint tell you about that nigga back there?"

"Hell yeah! Starr aint cause no harm to me, and it really wasn't shit."

"Aite you damn Jolly Green Giant, don't be raising yo voice and shit at me, I aint Kenzie nigga."

"You and yo girl with these giant jokes, aint my fault y'all short as hell." We rode back to my house laughing and joking, and he left when he got to his car. I walked in the condo and it was quiet, except for the sound of the tv that was turned down. Kenzie was sleep in her bassinet and Kiarra was on her phone typing away, and laughing.

"Who you talking to?" She looked at the me funny

and sat up on the couch.

"When do you start asking me that? I'm talking to Lo and Kodi in our group chat."

"I was just asking, is that a problem?"

"Is it something you want to get off your chest, because I'm not doing the guessing game, and you being weird as fuck right now."

"I saw Church." Her face balled up, and I saw her eye twitch a little.

"Ok, and what does that have to do with me?"

"Why the fuck—"

"Hold up Deontae, watch your mouth around my daughter, and when you're talking to me. Come to the room." She stood up and made sure Kenzie was ok before she walked to the back. Her ass was switching hard as hell, and I know she was doing that on purpose.

"Now what the hell is going on, because you come in here with yo chest poked out cursing and shit, so wassup?"

After she tried to have this whole 'oh don't talk to me like that' mess, she come to the room and turn into KiKi from the block.

"What you expect, this nigga come up to me talking how he just talk to you and he meant what he said. I wanted to knock him the fuck out, but I thought about you and Zi. Why wouldn't you tell me?"

"Tae, it wasn't like I was sneaking around. The first time I saw him after everything went down, he was in my backseat when I got off work. Then, the night I went into labor, he called me sounding suicidal, so I went to see what was going on. When I got there and saw it wasn't shit wrong with him, I was about to leave, and his baby mama came and we got into and my water broke. I was focused on our baby, not Church ass. I'm still not thinking about him bae, I don't need you questioning me."

"Put yourself in my shoes."

"I was already in your shoes, just like you neglected to tell me that you saw your ex." My eyes bucked and I tried to play it off.

"How you know that?"

"You were in my part of town Tae, and bitches are nosey and messy as hell."

"Why you didn't say anything?"

"Why didn't you say anything?" she made a face while she was mocking me and I had to laugh.

"You was pregnant, and I didn't want you to go crazy on me."

"I'm not crazy so shut up."

Kenzie started to whine so we walked back to the front, and I picked her up.

"She is going to be so spoiled, and you're going to regret it later watch."

"That's cool, she gone know she can get anything from me. That go for you too bae, all you gotta do is say the word baby."

"I got everything I want already."

"I do too, well except for my boy, but I'll wait a year or two."

She rolled her eyes and took Kenzie from me so she

could breastfeed her. She only been a mother for a few weeks but she looked like a champ.

Kenzie is lucky to have her... I am too.

TWENTY THREE

Kodi

The last few months, I had been in the studio non-stop and I had two singles on the radio now. Gerald had been working with me, and our personal relationship was going good too. He told me that him and his brothers killed Gates, and I can't say that I was mad. After all the abuse I dealt with over the years, it was nice knowing I could finally stop looking over my shoulder.

"What you over there thinking about?"

"Nothing, you're ready to go?"

"Yeah, come on."

We were all heading to Kiarra and Deontae's condo for her a birthday dinner. This is going to be the first time she let everyone come see Kenzie so I was extra thirsty. I loved babies and couldn't wait to have my own. I could've had 2 babies by now if Gates hadn't beat them out of me before they even got a chance to grow.

"You being too quiet, you sure you doing ok?" Gerald took his eyes off the road for a second and did that creepy deep stare he always do. I wonder if he was reading my mind for real.

"I'm just thinking about everything, I'm finally happy, and around people that actually care about me so it feels good." He rubbed my thigh, and continued driving.

Gerald was always a gentleman when we were together; he never let me open a door by myself, and he always asked me how I was feeling or if I was hungry... gotta appreciate the man that'll feed you.

***

We got to their condo, and I swear I was jealous right now. It was an open layout, and everything looked new and expensive. I think the balcony is what stole my heart, it had the perfect view of the city.

"Hey y'all thanks for coming."

"No problem, happy birthday boo." I gave her the gift we brought for her and went to see Kenzie who was up looking around in Deontae's arm.

"Ohmigod she is so adorable, let me go wash my hands."

Deontae pointed me to the bathroom, and I washed my hands before I came back and sat on the couch. when Deontae handed her to me she started to squirm around, and kept her eyes on her father.

"You hold her all day don't you?"

"Yeah I do, I can't help it though."

"I don't blame you, look at those eyes, it's like she's putting a spell on me."

Everybody laughed, and watched Kiarra's Hallmark movies while we waited for everyone else to get there.

When Ki's mom and her boyfriend showed up right along Lo's parents, we took our seats at the table to eat.

Watching Kiarra and Lauren with their mom had me wishing I had a relationship with mine. She just cut me off because I wouldn't leave Gates, and because she hated my father; but that's another story for another chapter. I wanted to reach out, but I felt like she should be the one to do it, after all I am her daughter.

"Kodi, yo ass creeping me out staring off into space and shit."

"Nah, I was just thinking about my mom, I haven't talked to any of my family in a few years."

"You wanna go out there?"

"Yeah, but I don't think I can do it alone."

"I got you, just let me know and I'll move some stuff around." He was smacking on his chicken and licking his finger, and I was ready take his plate away.

"What's wrong?"

"Yo ass over there smacking like a cow, that's what's wrong, close yo damn mouth." Lauren beat me to the punch and everybody laughed at Gerald.

"Shut up midget, you aint funny."

"I aint tryna be funny." She playfully rolled her eyes and went back to drinking her wine. Lauren was a little wino, every time we hung out she was bringing out a big bottle of wine.

Kenzie started getting fussy, so Kiarra took her to the back to feed and change her diaper.

"Ok, so in case you all didn't know, I'm proposing to Kiarra tonight."

"Aaaawwwww."

"Lauren shut up you knew already."

"Aw yeah… it's still sweet so, aaawwww."

"Well, I need y'all help to make it go."

"What you need bro?"

"I need somebody to find *Happily Ever After by Case* and play it through the speakers. Lo, take Kenzie and change her into this onesie. That's it, I'll take care the rest of it."

"Omg I think imma cry, my baby getting married, I'm not ready for this."

"Mama Mel, get yourself together."

I'm so excited for Kiarra, she deserves all of this.

"You look like you about to cry and shit."

"Shut up Gerald, I am not about to cry." I wiped my face when he turned around and tried to act normal when Ki came back out. Everybody looked so obvious, and I was trying so hard not to laugh.

TWENTY FOUR

Kiarra

Ever since I came back from changing Kenzie everybody was acting weird. My mom looked like she was about to cry, and if they were about to tell me something was wrong, I was going to lose it.

"What's wrong with y'all?"

"I want my God baby, that's what's wrong with me." Lo came and got Kenzie from me and start rocking her as she walked away.

"You ready to open your gifts baby?"

"Sure, let me see what I got."

I opened my gifts, and half of them was stuff for Kenzie, or gift cards to a baby store.

"Thank y'all so much I love it, even though this look like Kenzie's birthday."

"Uuuhhh Ki, Ken Ken just spit up on her clothes, I'll go change her." Lo went to Kenzie's room and Banks started playing music.

"You bet not be tryna plug yo mixtape bro, we heard it already." Gerald said causing everybody to erupt in laughter

"Fuck you Gerald, don't be hating on me man."

"Here, come get this spitting mama."

I grabbed Kenzie and looked at the shirt she had on. It just said, 'Will You' on it, and I know I never seen it before.

"Who bought her this shirt bae?"

Guess what I did today. those
were the words I said to you.

It was last May, don't know the exact
day. in my head there was a praise.

I turned around to look at Deontae and he was on one knee. It felt like the wind was knocked out of me as he grabbed my left hand.

And I asked you, would you do me,
the honor of being my wife?

I was at a loss for words as I tried to focus on breathing, and not dropping my baby.

"Kiarra Jordyn Walker, I love you so much, and I want to know if you would do me the honor of being my wife?"

"Yessss you know I will, Ma hold my baby." My mama was laughing with tears streaming down her face, and I held my hand out for Deontae to put the ring on.

The 2ct rose gold diamond ring had me speechless. My heart felt like it was in my stomach, and I was crying like a baby.

"Aaawww, congratulations y'all, imma be the flower girl." Lo hugged me and held my hand out to look at the ring. "Girl you gone have to watch yo back before you getting bussed upside the head for this."

"Girl I swear, them jack boys gon' be lurking." Kodi said as she hugged me and looked at the ring.

"Kodi what you know about jack boys? Let me find

out."

Everyone stayed until it was time for to put Kenzie to bed. Once she was fed and changed, she went right to sleep, and I went to bed to cuddle with my fiancé'. He was sitting on the ottoman watching clips on Sports Center when I walked in, and he turned the tv off when I laid in the bed.

"Did you enjoy your birthday baby girl?"

"Yes, I did, thank you for that, I think this was one of the best birthdays ever."

"I'm glad I can do that for you baby. How do you feel with me going back to work in 2 weeks?"

"It's going to tough adjusting to doing everything alone, but I'll call one of our moms to help if I need it."

"Let's go get married tomorrow or something."

"How are we going to do that?"

"We can go to the court house, unless you really want a big wedding."

"No, not really, we can just have a big reception."

"So, it's set we gone go get our license tomorrow?"

"Yeah!"

"Good, now send out a text and tell everybody get their Sunday's best out the closet."

"I love you Deontae."

"I love you too baby girl, go to bed."

I cuddled against his body and drifted off to a peaceful slumber. In a couple of days, I'll be Mrs. Blak, and couldn't be happier.

TWENTY FIVE

Gerald

"Turn the bass up a little G."

"I got you bro."

Banks was in the studio finishing his album, and he was just about done besides the song he was doing now. I was supposed to be going to Lafayette with Kodi tomorrow so I was going to be in the studio all night to finish up what I could.

"That shit sound good as hell bro." Banks stepped out the booth and grabbed his bottle of water.

"Yeah it was, I know this gon' be the album that take you to the top."

"Appreciate it bro."

"Knock, knock. Oh, hey Gio, that was you I heard? It sounded good." Some chick that resembled Olivia from G unit came walking in the studio.

"This a closed session, you gotta step out."

"She good G, wassup Nicki?" Banks start licking his lips, and I excused myself from the room because I didn't want any parts of Lauren when she found out; her lil' ass was crazy. I called to check on Kodi, and she answered sounding like she was running a marathon.

"Hey bae."

"Girl what the hell you doing?"

"I'm in the gym on the treadmill."

"When you start working out?"

"Shut up, I'm tryna be healthy. And I'm nervous as hell about tomorrow, my mother can be a bit… extra."

"Don't trip bae, I got yo back, you know that." The Nicki chick walked out the room fixing her top and re-applying lipstick. I walked back in shaking my head at Banks.

"What?"

"Lo gone beat yo ass if she finds out."

"Find out what? I aint did shit."

"Aite, that aint my business." I sat at the computer and he got back in the booth. If it aint concerning this music, I aint worrying bout it.

****

We were driving the 2 hours to Lafayette, Indiana, and I was happy as hell it didn't snow last night.

Kodi was nervously bouncing her leg as we drove on I-65 South.

"Calm down before yo ass throw up or something."

We pulled up to her mom's house, and there were a few cars parked outside. "She must be having Thanksgiving here, Ohmigod, that mean everybody is here."

I got out the car and opened her. She took my waiting hand and stepped out the car. The front door opened, and Kodi looked like she just seen a ghost.

"Are my eyes deceiving me is that my stubborn little Kodi?"

Kodi dropped her head, and I lifted it back up. "You good baby, ignore that negative shit, you came here to try to squash shit. If she doesn't accept the shit, then we going home, and hitting up Deontae mom's house for dinner. Shit we might stop by anyway, she said she was going to make me a caramel cake."

"You're so fat Gerald."

She led me to the house, and we walked up the 6 steps that led to the front door.

"How are you doing ma'am? Happy Thanksgiving, I'm Gerald." I held my hand out for her to shake and she looked down at it, and back up to my face.

"Why are you here?"

"Let's go Gerald."

"No, it's cool baby." I turned my attention back to her mother and looked her directly in the eye.

"I'm sorry I didn't get your name ma'am?"

"Just call me Rebecca."

"Ok, Rebecca, I came here so that my girl Kodi can make things right with her family. I care about her deeply and I'll do anything to make her happy. For whatever reason, she actually cares if she has a relationship with her family. If you don't accept that, then we'll calmly leave your property and drive that 2 hours back to Chicago."

She stood there with her arms folded, and another woman that resembled Kodi came to the door. "Hi, I'm Kodi's big sister Koryn, it's nice to meet you, come on in. I'm glad you came back Kodi."

We walked in the house, and her mouth just mumbled some words under her breath, and went to the kitchen. I'm making sure I make all my plates, or I gotta be there when it's made. This bitch look like she'll do some disrespectful shit that'll have me shooting her in her pinky toe or sumn.

I know Kodi was mixed, but this house was packed with white people, I guess her pops people wasn't joining the festivities.

"Heyyy Kodi, it's been so long, you're looking good."

People were hugging her and she looked uncomfortable, or scared. She kept looking back at me, and I just stood in the background unless somebody said something to me.

Rebecca gave me the stink eye all damn night, and I was ready to tell her ass to throw dem hands real shit.

"So, Gerald, is it? What exactly do you do for a living?"

"I'm a music producer."

"Oh, really. Is that all you do?"

I wanted to tell her ass I smack disrespectful bitches for a living but I settled with. "Yeah, that's it."

"Rebecca, you need to stop treating him like that, he has been a gentleman and I think I like him for Kodi, she actually looks happy." Her sister spoke up Koryn came to my defense, and Rebecca looked like she mentally killed her two times.

"I can do whatever the hell I want in my damn house, if he doesn't like it, then he can go, the front door haven't moved."

"Come on Gerald, I'm trying to be respectful, but imma end up dragging my own mother, let's go. Koryn, you have my number, call me if you want to talk."

I pulled Kodi's chair back, and we walked towards

the front door, but her mom yelled behind us and made Kodi halt her steps.

"Yeah, get the hell out of here! She could've stayed gone, I never wanted her mutt ass anyway!"

"Fuck this." Kodi turned around and tried to rush her mom but I picked her up and carried her out the house.

"Put me down Gerald, let me go back in there plea-seee." Her face was turning red and she had tears running down her face. I put her in the car and put her seatbelt on.

"If you get out this car, me and you are going to have some problems. You understand?"

I closed her door and jogged around to the driver's side. Kodi was crying and punching my dash board.

"Why do she hate me like it's my fault who my father is? Because I'm half black, she treats me like shit and always have. That's why I couldn't wait to get the hell away from here. Thank you for coming Gerald. I don't know what I would've done."

"You don't have to thank me baby, I told you I had your back."

"I'm glad we met, I love that you don't judge me off my past."

"We all got a past baby, but you going places. You didn't stay down, and let that sucka nigga change your heart; you dusted yourself off, and came back swinging."

"You just saying all the right things, must be tryna get some."

"I mean, shiiiiitt if you giving it to me, imma take that shit." We haven't had sex, and I wasn't rushing it, because I wanted more that something physical with Kodi.

"Well, get back to my place, and we can do that."

I start doing 90 on the expressway, and Kodi was in the passenger seat laughing. She don't know what she getting herself into.

TWENTY SIX

Lauren

It was the day of Kiarra and Deontae's reception, and I was proud of my work. Well the work of the people I hired. Deontae was set to go back to work tomorrow, so they wanted to do it today. Of course, yours truly was taking care of all the pictures, but I also hired some another photographer for when I just want to party.

Everyone one was dancing and having a good time, when I saw Banks' ex hoe Nicki come strutting in the damn venue and right up to him.

I walked up and he was trying to push her off of him.

"Come on you tweaking, you gotta go."

"You're the one who told me it was ok if I came."

"Is that right Giovanni? And when did you two have this conversation that I didn't know anything about?"

"It wasn't shit Lo, come on let's go over here." Gio tried to touch my arm but I looked down at his hand and raised my eyebrow so he took his hand and ran it down his face.

"We've been in contact for a while now, I thought you two were broken up."

"I aint never tell you no shit like that g stop lying."

"But, you admit that it was a conversation?"

"Can we talk about this later, why we gotta do this here?"

"We absolutely cannot talk about this later. She's here right now, so we gone do this shit right now."

"Since you acting like a cat got your tongue… me and Gio have been kicking it, and we had sex a few times, aint that right?"

I looked over at Banks, and he was looking everywhere but at me. "We can go outside now, let's talk."

I was calm, but little did they know, the second we got outside I was whopping both of their asses. I saw Kiarra following me outside, and I had to laugh, because this girl was dolled up, with an expensive ass dress on, but she knew what I was on, so she was riding with me.

"Can we talk without no bullshit out here?"

"Yeah hold on."

BAM!

I hit Nicki first and I was being pulled back immediately, but Kodi jumped right in and was whooping her as. I didn't even know she came outside but I was glad she did. I turned my attention back to Gio and he was looking pissed, but I can guarantee he wasn't madder than I was.

"What did I tell you Gio?"

"Come on Lo, it wasn't even shit she just gave me head."

"You know what, I'm not gone give you the satisfaction of me acting a fool out here. Don't even think about calling, texting, or emailing me. Imma send you all of your proofs and I'm done."

I walked back into the reception with Ki and Kodi following behind me. Gio stayed behind to help that bitch up and it made me want to go back and stomp him down there with her.

"You ok Lo?"

"I'm good boo, where is Ken Ken, I miss her little chocolate face." I went to get Kenzie from Deontae, and he was looking like he wanted to say something, but he just kept his mouth closed and continued to watch Kiarra.

I was starting to feel like it was something wrong with me, this was the second nigga that played me. Like I know I was a little crazy, but I wasn't that bad, in my eyes anyway.

After the reception, I helped Ki take their gifts home and I went home to soak, and drink my wine. I couldn't sleep so I got all of Banks proofs together like I said and emailed them to him.

Banks: *You really not even gon' do business with me Lo?*

I didn't even bother responding as I put him on the DND list.

Now that I think about it, the problem aint me, it's the men I date, I need to leave them light skinned niggas alone and find me some dark chocolate.

*****

After me and Banks broke up, I buried myself in my work, and I even bought me a condo down the street from Kiarra.

"My Gbaby need to be on billboards, look at her." Ki had brought Kenzie over to have her first photo shoot and we just finished.

"You so silly, how you been though?"

"Shit busy making money, Holiday time is the best for me."

"I mean with the whole Gio cheating thing?"

"What about it? Fuck that nigga, I'm good, shit I'm blessed."

"Really Lo?"

"Yes really, you know my bounce back game strong. I mean it's a fucked up situation, but I'm not about to sit around and cry about it when I could be stacking my bread."

"Don't try to hold in your feelings, I know you had real feelings for him, it's been a year."

"Ookaaayyy, is this a counseling session or a photo shoot?"

"Well, excuuuussseeee me! It's time for us to go take our daily nap anyway."

I helped Ki to the car, and she drove the few blocks over to her place. You know when you leave somebody that you used to spend all your free time with, so now you're bored as hell because you don't have nothing else to do? Yeah that's me right now scrolling through *Facebook* and *Snapchat* trying to find a party to go to or something.

"Hello?"

"Hey boo, what you doing?" I decided I wanted to do some Christmas shopping, and called Kodi to see if she wanted to go with me.

"Nothing, my sister is supposed to be on her way out here."

"Y'all wanna go shopping with me?"

"You wanna do my shoot for my mixtape cover?"

"If you paying bitch yeah."

"Duh I'm paying Lo, I'll let you know when I want it. Sooo, you know I don't have a car, are you gon' meet us at my house."

"Yeah, but you driving just so you know."

"Ugh I knew it was something, ok see you soon."

I hung up and grabbed my purse so I could leave out.

****

Kodi wanted to go to start our shopping on Roosevelt, and her sister Koryn was clutching her purse looking scared as hell.

"Girl relax, you make me want to rob yo ass the way you holding on to that bag."

We had just walked into *Mago Grill & Cantina* for lunch, and I ordered me two shots of *1800* as soon as we were seated. If I had to listen to Koryn complain about one more thing, I was going to scream... then choke the hell out of her.

The waiter came to take our food orders, of course Kodi and I knew what we wanted already. But, leave it to aggy ass Koryn to ask a million questions about how the food was prepared.

"Koryn, order a damn salad and move on, I'm hungry, and you irritating as hell. Matter fact, I'm moving to another table, so can you go put my order in first? I'm not with they ass."

"Wow Kodi, your friend is very animated."

"Bitch, what's animated is that lace front. Whoever did that shit need they ass whooped, yo shit go from eyebrows straight to yo wig, fuck is yo forehead at bruh?" Kodi laughed as I ranted and grabbed all my shit off the table.

"Talking about I'm animated, no hoe, I'm starving because you want to ask dumb ass questions." I sat at an empty table and texted Kiarra.

Me: *G… I'm never going out with Kodi's sister again this bitch is irrrrraaaa*

Kiarra: *be nice Lo!*

Me: *That ship has sailed… but I didn't hit her so*

My food came out, so I ate in peace by myself. Kodi and her sister took an Uber back to her house and I was dancing in my damn seat. I ate them and finished walking down Roosevelt to find something else to do. The smell of *Garett's Popcorn* had me going in to buy me a few bags. When I tell you, this is the best popcorn ever, I mean it!

There was a new tattoo shop that opened on near my studio, so that was my next stop. My skin was bare because my daddy would kill me; but I'm feeling like a rebel today.

I parked in the lot assigned to the building, and walked into the spacious shop. It was empty, except for the guy sitting behind the receptionist desk, but the artwork on the wall was amazing.

"Welcome to *Chi Ink*, do you have an appointment?"

"Nah, not really, I was kinda hoping you take walk ins?"

"I'll see it's been super busy today." I did another scan of the empty shop and he laughed.

"I'm fucking with you, what you tryna get today?"

"I really don't know."

"Ummm, ok. What type of stuff do you like?"

"I'm a photographer, so my camera is my baby... and I like seahorses."

"Cameras and seahorses, I got you. Now where do you want this? My name is Adonis by the way." Adonis held his hand out for me to shake, and I admired all the tattoos he had on his forearm.

"I'm Lauren, and I'll figure out where I want it once I see what it is. How long you been over here?"

"A couple months, but shit is slow as you can see."

"You need to work on your marketing. I lowkey only knew about it because my studio is on the top floor, but I like the feel in here."

"Well plug me then, and I'll give you a deal on this piece I'm working on."

I took my jacket off, and got my *iPhone 8* out my back pocket. Adonis asked for a picture of a vintage camera, so I showed him, and he got busy sketching my tattoo. I made sure my hair and everything was in place before I went live on *Facebook.*

"Hey y'all its ya girl Lo diddy, and I'm here with Mr. Adonis at *Chi Ink* about to get my first tattoo. Say hi to the people Adonis."

"Wassup y'all, everybody come check me out at

2150 Canalport ave, I'm on the 5th floor, open as late as I need to be."

"So, tell us about yourself, how long have you been tattooing?"

"I've been into art since I was able to hold a pencil, then I started painting, and now, I'm using my talent for a more permanent canvas."

"Well, there you go, I'm signing out, and I'll check back in when I'm done." I blew a kiss in the camera and ended the live.

"Now, how much of a deal do I get with this?"

"I got you don't worry about that, you ready?" I looked at the sketch and my breath was taken away. He drew a vintage Polaroid One Step, that had a picture falling from it.

"I love that! I want it right here on my side, but add some more falling pictures."

"This yo first tattoo, you can come back for that. Come on to the back." I followed him to a private room, and laid down on the table.

"You're going to need to take your shirt off."

"Aw naw, imma have to charge you to do my tattoo, I aint got no bra on."

"I aint got no bra on either, we even. Stop being scary, yo titties aint even that big Ma."

I took my sweater off and he put some type of paper on my nipples.

"Some people don't like to hear the sound of the machine buzzing the entire time so you can go to Pandora and pick some music."

"What type of music you listen to Adonis?"

"I'm fucking with GHerbo right now."

"Ok, ok, I can agree on that, his *Humble Beast* mixtape go kinda hard."

I picked GHerbo Pandora station, and watched Adonis as he put gloves on, and opened a new pack of needles. If I wasn't scared of needles before, I definitely was now. He put the sketch down and I closed my eyes as I felt the needle pierce my skin.

"You gotta breathe or you gon' pass out Lauren."

I just nodded my head up and down tried to remember how to breathe.

"Talk to me, what made you want to come in and get tatted today?"

"You need to focus, and leave me alone."

"I'm focused trust me."

It took 2 and a half hours for Adonis to finish the tattoo, and I couldn't even feel my side anymore. He helped me stand up and I walked to the full length mirror he had in the hall.

"Ohmigod, I love this! You did great, I love the detail in the camera, it looks so real."

"You aint gotta gas me up, I was gon' give you my number already."

"Boy!" we laughed together and I got my phone so I could go live again.

"Lo diddy is baaaacccckkk! And bruh man from 5th floor did his thang on my tat!"

Adonis was behind me laughing and cleaning the

area up as I showed off my tattoo in the mirror.

"Aite I'm gone, don't forget to come check Adonis out at *Chi Ink*. Are you on social media?"

"Yeah I'm on *Instagram* and *Facebook* @ChiCityInk follow me."

I ended the video, and got back dressed so I could leave. "How much do I owe you?"

"It's on the house, you just gotta go on a date with me."

"Well, I'm not interested in dating, so you can take this $300 and call it a day, or I'm just leaving."

"Damn, we couldn't just go out to eat as friends?"

"You aint slick, thanks for hooking me up though." I walked out the room, and put the money on the front desk, before I left out to go home.

Tomorrow I'm going to get my hair cut, the glow up about to be real.

TWENTY SEVEN

Church

Shit was going all bad for me; personally, and with my business. Ever since my nigga Gates got whacked, niggas been slipping on their job. Right now, Tre set up meeting with all of the workers, and the it was about 20 niggas sitting around the table waiting for me or Tre to say something.

I stood up to start talking when Tre pulled out his heat and shot one of the lil' niggas Greg in his head.

Pow!

"Now, shit been short, and I need to know who the fuck this it's a fucking game?"

"Fuck you shoot him for?"

"I aint like the way that nigga was breathing, shit was suspect as fuck. Like I was saying tho."

Tre turned back around and everybody sat with a blank face except one person. I watched Flip the entire time, and he refused to look me in the eye.

"Shit about to change up, if I gotta kill every last one of you niggas, that's what the fuck is going to happen. I'll be calling with instructions soon." Tre dismissed the meeting, and they ass was moving fast like they had to be home before the street lights came on.

"That nigga Flip know something, imma have somebody keep an eye on him."

"You should've had that nigga get this body outta here."

"You did that shit, so you on yo own, I'm out."

I left out the building, and got in my car to go home. To keep from hearing Miranda bitch about everything under the sun, I had been staying in a lot.

"Bout time you showed up, MJ don't want to go to sleep, and I'm tired, so here."

"Fuck you tired from, you don't do shit all day?"

"I take care of your kids all day, that's a lot!"

"Bitch, they in daycare majority of the day, so try again with that lie."

"Why do you gotta disrespect me in front of son Church. What you mad that your one true love is married?"

"Fuck you talking about?"

"Guess you didn't know… oops." Miranda tried to walk away but I snatched her back by her hair.

"Keep playing, and imma snatch the rest of yo fucking edges out." I let her go and she ran upstairs.

I put MJ in his play pen and stalked Kiarra's social media. My blood was boiling as I scrolled through all the pictures of her and Deontae.

"Daddy?" Mia came from behind me and climbed in my lap.

"Why you not sleep baby?"

"I'm hungry, can I have some ice cream?"

"I'll take you get some ice cream tomorrow, it's too late right now."

"Ooohh is that Mama Ki? I miss her daddy."

"I do too. G so back to bed baby before we have to

hear yo mama's mouth."

"Ok, love you."

"Love you more."

Mia ran off to her room, and I stayed up all night staring at pictures of Kiarra in her wedding dress. I remember when Ki used to drop hints that she wanted to get married, and I turned her down every time... now I'm wishing I would've just did it, and this nigga Deontae living life with my girl, and a baby that should've been mine.

I walked down to the basement, where I kept my personal stash. I made me two perfect lines of cocaine, and rolled up a hundred dollar bill from my pocket. The first line I did sent me into an instant state of euphoria and I was floating on the clouds by time I did the second one. When I had enough time to get myself together, I went upstairs to fins Miranda sitting up in bed. I could've sworn she said she was going to sleep.

"I'm not going to keep coming 2nd to a bitch who don't even want you. If you take all that energy and give it to me, we could be happy."

I said a quick prayer before I had to choke the snot out of her ass. "Listen, you need to go the fuck to sleep real shit."

She got out the bed, and stood in front of me with her hands on her hips. "If shit don't change, I'm taking my kids and we're leaving."

"Didn't you just leave and brought yo ass right back?"

"You're taking me for granted, Church don't be mad when I move on."

"I'm not taking yo ass nowhere, go find somebody so you can leave me the fuck alone."

"How could you say that to meeee?!" Miranda started her dramatics and was on her knees like she was praying.

"Shut the fuck up before you wake my kids up. Get off the floor ma, what you want Miranda?"

"I want to get married."

My high was instantly blown. I barely wanted her ass to be my baby mama, fuck I look like marrying her? I walked around her and went into our private bathroom. I told the shower on and she came stomping behind me.

"Really Marshall, you can't marry me, but I can have your kids? That's fucked up, I bet if Kiarra asked you to marry her, you'll turned the world upside down to make it happen.

"You fucking right! I would marry Kiarra in a fucking heartbeat, but I aint marrying yo rat ass! Yo ass was happy being a side bitch, as long as you had a piece of me. You think that's the type of bitch I want to marry? No! Now get the fuck out this bathroom Miranda!" She ran out crying like Red from *Friday* after Debo snatched his chain, and I closed the door.

Every time we got into an argument, her ass was bringing Kiarra up, she wanted me to hurt her damn feelings.

When I got out the shower, Miranda wasn't in the room, and I figured she went to lay on the couch, like always did when she had an attitude.

I peeked in Mia's room, and I didn't see her in the bed. "Miranda! Miranda, Mia down there with you?"

I walked down the stairs, and it was quiet as hell, besides the tv that was on. MJ wasn't in his crib, and that's when I noticed her purse and car keys was gone.

This bitch gone make me kill her.

TWENTY EIGHT

Kodi

It was Christmas Eve, and instead of being surrounded around friends and family, I was at home in the den recording some songs. Gerald helped me sound proof the walls, and it was set up like my own little mini studio. I even had a love seat in here for when I wanted to sit in her and write. All I was missing was a piano, and I found the perfect one; the only problem was, it was $1,800, and I already broke the bank getting my studio together.

Hey Kodi, are you coming to Mother's house tomorrow?

I laughed when I saw the text from Koryn, if she thought I was going to come out there again, she was out of her mind.

Closing the message, I went to *Facebook* and sang *While We're Young* while I was on live.

Saaang girl!

You cute boo!

Kiarra and Lauren were the first to comment, then it was hundreds of comments that came flooding in.

Bing!

Gerald texted me and I was smiling like Cheshire cat

Moms wanna know if you coming over tonight... I miss you

I miss you too

Come over

No spend that time with your family, I'll see you when you done

I'll bring you a plate

Gerald told me his family always celebrate Christmas on Christmas Eve, because it was rare that his sister had the day off. Being with Gerald helped me realize that there was still some gentleman around. He always told me how beautiful I was, and sent me sweet texts when he had to be in the studio all day. It was the little things that mattered to me.

Not really in the mood to record anymore tonight, I shut down everything and laid across the couch binge watching *Shameless*. If I had a father like Frank Gallagher, I think I would be worse than I already was.

Open the door

Gerald texted me so I got up and unlocked the front door for him.

"Wassup baby, what you in here doing?"

"Waiting on this food, I was about to die." I took the bag from him and sat on the floor with my food.

"This my shit what season you on? Fiona ass be bussing it open for everybody."

"Shut up! I'm only on season 6."

"My bad, what's your plans for tomorrow?"

"I don't know, Ki invited me to over to their house, so imma go over there with them."

"Hell yeah! I hope Tae moms cooking, we in there bae."

"You wasn't invited Gerald I was."

"Wherever you invited I'm invited too fuck you talking bout? And I knew them before you, how you just gone say I wasn't invited?"

"You mad or nah?"

"Nah I aint… I'm sleepy as hell though, I'm bout to go lay in your bed."

"You better not get in my bed with those clothes on."

"Don't trip, imma be butt ass naked."

"Well I'm coming with you then."

"Yo lil' nasty ass tryna get some Christmas D huh?"

I followed Gerald to the room, and we went for hours trying to set a new record. With Gates, I never wanted to have sex, and I always had to hold in my throw up when he was on me. Now, I was like a nympho I couldn't get enough of Gerald.

****

Christmas morning we stayed in bed until it was time to get dressed. Gerald had a bag in his trunk, so he got dressed at my house and we drove the 20 minutes to Ki's condo.

When we got there and I saw Banks with the girl I had to beat up at Ki's reception, I was ready to tag her again, because she had a lot of nerves coming here.

"Yo ass better not be fighting and shit today, don't even walk passed her." Gerald smacked me on my butt and I sat next to Ki who was rocking Kenzie to sleep.

"Who the hell invited her?"

"The bitch came with Banks, and Tae won't let me kick him out."

"Did you tell Lo?"

"Yeah, she said she didn't care, so we will see… you never know with her."

Lauren walked in looking like Joanne the Scammer with this fur on and this blonde wig, and I was dying laughing at her.

TWENTY NINE

Lauren

I had my petty pants on today since Banks wanted to play by bringing this bitch to my best friend house, like he didn't know I was going to be here.

"Merry Christmas everybody! What you over there laughing at Kodi?"

"Where you get that fur from?"

"Oohh don't be hating, you know I look good." I flipped my wig and found me a seat at the table.

"Where my Kenny boo at?"

"She sleep bestie, why are you in looking like you about sit courtside of a boxing match?"

"Because I'm tapping into my inner petty, you gone see."

"Don't have nothing popping off in my house."

"Oh baby, you know I don't disrespect nobody's home, on purpose anyway." When Ki texted and told me Banks brought this bitch, I texted Adonis and invited him over. It's not like we had anything going on, but Banks aint know that. and I was about to ruffe some feathers.

"Merry Christmas Lo, you wasn't gone speak to me?" Banks had the balls to come sit next to me.

"Ha!"

"I got you something for Christmas."

Silence

"You not gon' say shit?"

"Giovanni, why would you just leave me over there by myself?"

Hearing Nicki's voice had me ready to turn this Christmas dinner to Tables, Ladders, and Chairs match.

I'm outside.

"I'll be back Ki."

I went downstairs to meet Adonis, and when he saw me he was bent over laughing. "G what happened to yo head?"

"Aint nothing happen to my head, this is a wig, why you hating on me?"

"I aint hating on you, I hate that rat on yo head, it's crooked as hell." I playfully punched him in the arm and he followed me in the condo.

When we walked back into the family room, all eyes were on us. Kiarra shook her head and looked at Deontae, who was looking at Banks.

"This what the fuck you do now Lo?" He walked up to me with his nostrils flared and I had a satisfying grin on my face.

"You better move around, and worry about yo girl, she over there looking real bothered Banks."

I walked around introducing Adonis to everybody, then everybody starting exchanging gifts. Of course Kenzie had majority of the presents that was under the tree, and her lil' 2 month old butt didn't even know what was going on.

"You using me bro?" We had just finished eating, and the caterer Ki hired was cleaning up.

"What you talking about?"

"Why you really ask me here?"

"Because I wanted to spend time with my friend, is that a problem?"

"You full of shit, but I gotta go pick my daughter up, you riding with me?"

"Oh no, I'm about to stuff my face with sweet potato pie, then go home to pass out."

"Aite walk me out." Adonis said bye to everybody and I walked him down to his car.

"Be safe driving."

"Aite Lo." Adonis hugged me and his *Gucci Guilty* cologne filled my nose, and had me hugging him a minute longer than I was supposed to. He gave me a peck on my lips, got in his car, and drove off.

As I turned around to go back inside the building, Banks and Nicki walked out, and she stomped all the way to his car. He fixed his lips to say something to me and I held my hand up to stop him.

"Whatever you're about to say, save it."

"Why you being so petty? You just gone bring other niggas around when you know I was gon' be here?"

"Banks I'm not about to be waiting out here!"

"Well bitch walk, you see me talking!"

"Bye Banks, we have nothing else to talk about."

What is it with niggas trying to profess their love when you don't give a shit anymore? But, when they had you, motha fuckas took you for granted. If I wanted a fuck boy, I'll get back with Tre, and that's a definite hell naw!

THIRTY

Kiarra

Life with a newborn has been crazy! Kenzie was spoiled as hell, thanks to her daddy, and I suffer when he's gone. Like now, Kenzie was screaming at the top of her lungs, and I was so tired. Thankfully, my mama volunteered to keep Kenzie, because she said she wanted to bring in the new year with her grandbaby.

Today is also Tae's birthday, and I wanted to do something special for him tonight.

In between surgeries wyd?

Packing Zi's bag

Aaww my baby really leaving me

We finally have some alone time

Oh shit I almost walked outta here…being paged love you wife

Love you too

I was smiling as I grabbed outfits for Kenzie. She was in her bouncer following me with her big hazel eyes. I love that even though she looks exactly like Deontae, she still have something of mine. We did a good job with this little girl. it had me thinking what our son would like.

PFFFFFFFFFFFFTPT!

Kenzie made the nastiest sounded fart, and I knew it was a mess in her diaper.

"Ohhh you stinky mama, you made a mess back there, didn't you? It's because you know you're leaving, I know your kind little girl."

The doorbell sounded, and I saw my mom from the camera app on my phone. I buzzed her in, and picked Kenzie up to change her shitty diaper.

"Is that my grandbaby smelling like that? I think I change my mind about taking her."

"No, Ma, you already here, I will chase you to your house with her."

"You shouldn't even do my grandbaby like, she wanna get away from you too, aint that right ma ma?"

I was wiping shit from her back, and my mama wanted to be all in her face playing. It's funny the things grandparents do you're their grandbabies. I caught my mama putting the skin off Kenzie's foot in her mouth, and I wanted to throw up. All she had to say was shut up, and that was good luck.

"Here you go, all clean you about to leave mommy now?"

My mama took her from me, and went to back all the bags of frozen breastmilk I had for her.

"She so little, you need to give her a little cereal."

"Mama if you give my baby some cereal we gon' have some problems."

"Fine, yo mammy aint no fun ma ma."

I gave Kenzie a million kisses before I put her in her car seat, and helped my mama outside with her.

"Don't call me Kiarra, I will block you if I have to."

"That's petty, I have a right to check on my baby."

"Try me if you want to. Love you Chubbz." She got in the car and pulled off from the curb.

I walked back inside, and start cleaning up. the house wasn't a mess, but you mothers know what it's like when you have that one table that got everything you're gonna need for the day; because you refuse to get off the couch, or out the bed. That was definitely my life the last two months. It was considered a good day if I remembered to shower every day. One day it got so bad Deontae woke me up like "Bae I'll watch Kenzie if you want to shower." I would've been embarrassed if I wasn't up with his fussy daughter for two days straight.

When I finished straightening the living room, I took a thirty minute shower, I even washed my hair in the shower.

I stepped out the shower and stared at my body in the mirror. I was still a little thick from having Kenzie, and I wanted to stay this size, I looked good.

Grabbing my moisturizer from under the sink, I two strands twisted my hair and went to the room to put on a night gown. It was only noon, but I had plans to sleep up until Deontae got home about, which was about 7 or 8.

I put Lifetime on, and got comfortable under the covers. I think I was sleep before my head hit the pillow.

***

"Ki, wake up you snoring loud baby girl."

"I'm sorry, heyy baby, how was work?" I gave him a kiss as he took his scrubs off.

"It was cool bae, how was Kenzie? Did she look for me when she left?"

"Tae, she is 2 months, she wasn't looking for nothing. But she was fussy as always, then had a blowout right before my mama got here." he laughed and walked towards the bathroom.

"My baby know me, I know she looked for me. you coming in here with me?"

I got up quickly, and took my gown off, exposing my bare body. Deontae bit his lip and turned the shower on.

"You sexy as hell Ki, and yo booty got bigger."

"You sexy as hell too, especially when you're complimenting me."

Deontae picked me up and pinned me against the shower wall. His penis found its way to my slippery tunnel, and I gasped loudly when he entered me.

He growled in my ear, and started moving in and out of me slowly.

"This shit feel good as hell Ki, damn, it don't even feel like you just a baby."

I didn't know how to feel about that last comment. Like was he expecting me to be loose or something?

"Aahh shit!" Deontae sped up his pace, and was pounding me again the wall.

"I can't hold this shit no more Ki."

"Give it to me then daddy." Right after the words

left my mouth, Deontae had me smashed between him and wall while he breathed like a dragon in my ear.

"Deontae, I can't breathe," I struggled out.

"My bad baby." He put me on my feet, and smacked me on the ass.

"What're we getting into tonight?"

"I don't know, I don't really feel like leaving. We can turn the fireplace on, and watch a movie on the couch, I know you have to get up early."

"Thank you, baby girl, that sound perfect."

We washed each other's body, and rinsed off. Deontae turned the water off, and he helped me out the shower before he got out.

"You know what you wanna watch bae?"

"It don't matter Tae, it's your birthday, you pick."

"Don't judge me, but I wanna see Girl's Trip."

"Really?" I start laughing and snuggled up on my husband. Being with Deontae was different for me, but I love this man so much, I would do it all over again.

THIRTY ONE

Lauren

"5….4….3….2….1 Happy New Years!"

Adonis had a New Year's Eve Party at *ChiInk* so I was here supporting of course. It was actually packed in here, I know some of them are people from his neighborhood, and then his brother was here too. Aaron and Adonis's personality were complete opposites. Adonis was more laid back, but he knew how to turn up at the same time. On the other hand, Aaron was laid back too, but he was acting like it was going to kill him to have fun. I don't even think this nigga so much as tapped his damn foot to a song. He was fine as hell like his brother though.

"Happy New Years, you having fun?" Adonis wrapped his arm around my shoulder and passed me the blunt he had in his hand.

"Yeah, it's lit in here. When're you gon' add on to my tattoo?"

"Let me find out you addicted to tats now." Adonis smirked at me.

That was the truth though, the feel of the needle was therapeutic for me. "Yeah so what? Would you rather me be addicted to tattoos or crack?"

"Nigga." We both were laughing and smoking as the party went on around us. After it hit 3 in the morning, people started leaving to go eat, and I was right behind them.

"Damn you aint gon' help me clean up?"

"Hell naw, you better call a cleaning crew, I'm too tipsy for that shit."

"So how you getting home?"

"The same way I got here… my car."

"Naw, you been drinking too much, have a seat I'll drop you off."

"Yo ass was drinking too."

"You ain't see one glass to my lips, I smoke baby girl, I ain't no drinker."

I rolled my eyes and sat in a chair while the rest of the crowd dispersed. It took thirty minutes for the DJ to pack up his equipment, get paid, and leave. Then finally Adonis, Aaron, and me were leaving. Adonis locked the doors and dapped his brother up.

"You gon' be in later?" Adonis asked Aaron.

"Yeah, I got a 2 o'clock appointment, so I'm about to go pass out. Nice seeing you again Lauren."

"Same here, be safe."

Adonis walked to my car and walked to the driver's side. "Damn you ain't gon' open the door for me?"

"Yo hands ain't drunk, and you ain't my girl, so I'm not being a gentleman." I had a deep scowl on my face, and he laughed and came to open my door.

"I'm fucking with you Lo, come on."

"Yo black ass always tryna be funny." I pouted.

"I ain't even that black."

"Blacker than me."

"You racist as hell, and we the same damn race."

We had *Pandora* playing as he drove to my house. Adonis was cool to be around, and he when he wasn't busy, he let me use him as my muse when I want to test out different shots.

He pulled up to my condo, and we went inside. This isn't the first time he had to drive me home when I was drinking, and he usually stay in the guest room.

"When you stop playing and give me a real chance?"

"I'm not playing, I don't wanna be in a relationship right now, and we're good like this." I waved my finger between us.

"So you just wanna be friends with me? And you ain't gon' be mad if I start fucking with some boppers out here?"

"Bop away Adonis. Good night, if you leave before I get up… lock the bottom lock."

"I got you."

I went to my room and took a shower before I crawled under the covers. I uploaded all the pictures I took on *Facebook* and *Snapchat,* then scrolled through my timeline until I fell asleep.

The next day I didn't wake up until after noon, and that was only because Kodi called me back to back.

"Kodi, what the hell are you calling me so much for who the hell died?"

"Happy New Years! And nobody died I was just trying to see if you was still going to do my pictures."

"Yessss, omg you are a bug Kodi. When do you want it done?"

"I can come in Wednesday."

"You doing too much, I don't even know if the stylist I use is going to be free, I'll call you back…. I need to wake up before I talk business."

"Okay don't forget."

"Bye girl!"

I hung up and laid back down, then I heard footsteps coming down the hall. "I heard you up already, come on so you can take me to my car."

"Uuuuhhhh, take an Uber." I groaned rolling over in the bed.

"You lazy as hell, aite, I'll hit you up later."

"'Kay."

When he closed my door, I got up and went to the bathroom. Once I emptied my bladder, and handled my hygiene, I got on my phone and texted my personal stylist, who also did hair and makeup. This was the main reason I only used her, she was a damn one stop shop for real.

Wth?! How many styles do you need?

Idk however many styles you can come up by then... bring em

I sent Victoria a picture of Kodi, and she just replying with the eye rolling emoji and said ok. Now, that's taken care of, I'm going my ass back to sleep.

THIRTY TWO

Kodi

I was at home pacing back and forth trying to calm my nerves down. Gerald was supposed to be taking me to Lo's studio for my photoshoot, and I was waiting for him to get there.

Gerald: You ready?

Me: Yeah hurry up!

Gerald: Shut up big head, come out.

I grabbed my purse and ran out the door. Gerald was waiting outside with the passenger door open and I gave him a quick kiss before I got in.

"What you so nervous for? Hands sweating and shit."

"I never did a photoshoot before."

"You took a picture before, stop acting like you aint got it. I got an all-day appointment so, let me know when you done and I'll send you a Uber to come get you."

"I can't wait to buy me a damn car, I'm tired of giving Uber my money."

"Have you been saving?"

"I mean yeah, but I like to shop. I can probably find

something nice for like $10,000 and pay it off. Until I can buy me a Maserati or something."

"Let me know when you wanna go, and I got you."

We pulled up and Lauren had just got there and was walking in the building.

"Right on time, that's what I like to see. Hey Gerald, this is a closed set I hope you not trying to stay."

"Damn, it's like that did I get dumped too?"

"It's nothing personal, just don't need you taking up space." I laughed and Gerald gave her the middle finger before he pulled off.

Another car pulled up, and a girl was getting out with a bunch of bags in her hand. "My assistant went to get donuts and coffee; can I get some help with this stuff?"

"See, this is why I always call you, you know the way to my heart is food." Lauren walked to her car and grabbed some things, so I followed and did the same.

"Kodi… this is Victoria, Victoria… this is Kodi."

"Nice to meet you."

"Nice to meet you too. I'm going to get started on your hair and makeup first, and when my assistant bring the rest of the clothes, you can pick what you like."

Victoria got to work on my hair. Two hours later, my hair ad make up was done and I was looking like a brand new person. She added some weave in my hair and straightened so it was down my back. I was loving this new look, and I might decide to wear my hair straight more often.

Lauren had the green screen sat up, and after an hour of taking pictures, we were finally done.

"These are going to be cute, I'll have these to you as soon as possible."

"Thank you! I'm about to go change and get my Uber."

I went to the dressing room, and changed back into my jogging suit.

I'm done

Aite, bout to order yo Uber, you feel like doing a feature? I told him 5k for it

Helllll yeah! thank you!

You got it

I walked out the room and gave Lauren a hug. When I was leaving out the door, Lauren lil' boo, who she swear wasn't her boo, was walking in.

"Is Lauren busy?"

"No, we just finished up, you should be good to go in." He nodded and went inside, while I waited out for my ride to pull up. A text popped up from Koryn and I rolled my eyes so hard I thought they would've got stuck

Mom wants to know will you be coming to the family reunion in May?

Haha! Hell no

We are still your family Kodi, you can't blame us for everything

I can't tell I got family, it's still a no for me!

Beep! Beep!

I looked up and saw my Uber, so I got in the back of the Toyota Camry, and rode in silence to the recording studio.

I walked into the studio that Gerald already used, and he was there with another guy who was in the booth recording. The song sounded good and I nodded my head as I made it to Gerald and gave him a kiss on the cheek.

"Daaammmnnn, you look good as hell, I like yo hair like that ma."

"Thank you, I do too, I might get it like this more often."

I sat on the couch and waited for the guy to finish

up with his verse.

"Yo Red, this my girl Kodi, she's the singer I mentioned earlier."

"How you doing? I heard some of yo songs on the radio, and I fuck with that track you did with Banks."

"I appreciate that."

"Well, bae the hook is written already… read over it, you can put yo own little spin on it if you need to."

He handed me a paper, and I went into the booth. After a few takes, my part was done, and I waited at the studio until Gerald was ready to go. This was our normal routine for the most part, unless I didn't feel like being in the studio all day.

"Bae, yo man is backed up… wanna have a quickie before we leave?"

"Lock the door."

Gerald jumped up and locked the door, while I took my clothes off. He wasted no time taking one of my perky nipples into his mouth and my head went back as I welcomed the pleasure. He stood up and gave me a slow passionate kiss, before he picked me up and walked me to the couch. When he placed me on my feet, I got down on my knee and put his big monster in my mouth.

"Ssssss Fuck!" Gerald grabbed the back of my head and was moving me at the pace he wanted. I heard his toes popping, before I was being snatched up and threw on the couch. I got into position on my hands and knees and Gerald rammed himself inside of me. Usually Gerald was slow and sensual, but today he was going like he downed a fifth of Hennessey.

"Ahhhh shit!" I couldn't take it as pounded into me relentlessly. The only sounds you heard was skin slapping and moaning. Gerald buried his face and neck and sped his pace up. I felt his dick pulsating, so I knew he was about to cum. Seconds later he was growling in my ear and smacked me on the ass.

"Damn, bae, a nigga ready to go to sleep now." Gerald said as he chest heaved up and down.

"I am too and my damn hair sweating out already." He laughed and walked to the adjoining bathroom to get cleaned up.

We left and he drove us to my house, to finish what we started in the studio.

THIRTY THREE

Lauren

"Ki, where you at?"

"In my room!"

I followed her voice, and found her sitting on the bed looking like her puppy just got ran over.

"What's wrong with you?"

"He dun got me again bestie, I can't believe this shit."

"What?"

"I'm pregnant bitch!" I start dying laughing and Kiarra was looking like she wanted to beat my ass. "This is not funny! I think he did it on purpose."

"Girl you better shut up and have all yo husband's babies, at least you aint got fifty million baby daddies."

"I don't have a problem with having babies, but damn Kenzie isn't even one yet!"

"It's done now, this gon' be the son I wanted."

"You're not the one carrying this baby, you better tell Adonis to give you some of his secret sauce." She laughed and I playfully pushed her.

"Girl we are—"

"*Juuust Frriiieeennds* I know, you been saying that same lie for last 4 months or so."

"First of all, it's not a lie, and we are just friends, I don't know why everybody tryna make us be together. Mind ya business."

"Ok, ok I'll leave you and bae alone.

I got you a funnel cake from Sugar Shack, you better hurry up before I eat it.

I read Adonis's text and smiled. "Whatever, Ki, I gotta go."

"Mmmhhmmm, bae must be calling, bye."

"I hope Kenzie shit all on your favorite cover."

"You so petty." I laughed and walked out the door and down to my car.

Adonis was standing outside talking to somebody, and I thought it was just a client until she kissed him on the lips. I got out the car and his eyes met mine. I rolled my eyes and went into the building and up to my studio.

I heard the door alarm a couple minutes later and Adonis came in with a Styrofoam container. "I thought you would've waited downstairs for me."

"And why would I do that?"

"Damn, what's yo problem?"

"I don't have a problem what you mean?"

"Aite, well I got a client in like twenty minutes, but meet me downstairs when you done doing what you doing."

"Naw I'm good?"

"Why you iggin'? fuck wrong with you?"

"I told you I'm good."

"When you done with that little ass attitude, come downstairs."

"Alright, thanks for the funnel cake." He kissed his teeth and walked out the door.

I opened my laptop and sat Indian style in my comfy office chair. I had to finish touching up a few pictures from a shoot I had the other day, so that's what I was going to do.

*****

Come the fuck down here bro

I'm busy

You got 2 minutes or I'm hiding all yo edge control!

I jumped out my seat and ran out the door. I do not

play about my edge control, he was playing a dangerous game with me.

"I thought that'll get yo ass down here."

"What do you want Adonis? Hey Aaron."

"'Sup." He was sitting at his desk drawing as usual and didn't even look up when I walked in.

"Come to the back, I gotta show you something." He led me to one of his private room and all of his equipment was set up.

"You got a client coming or something?"

"Naw, lay down I'm bout to do the tattoo you been bugging me about." He showed me the pictures and it was a seahorse that had bubbles coming out of its mouth, and there was seashells surrounding it.

"Awww that's cute, and I aint paying you since you offered."

"Niggas boa… lay yo ass down."

"You don't even know where I want this at."

"You aint paying, you don't get to choose, now lay down and roll yo pants leg up."

I did what he said and laid still as he did my tattoo.

"Ooohhhh, I love iitttt."

"Yeah I know." Adonis took a picture of it on his phone and cleaned up his work area.

"What you about to get into Don?"

"Stop making up nicknames and shit. But, I got a date later on… other than that nothing."

"A date? With who?"

"My girl nigga, who else?"

"Mmm. Well, have fun."

"Don't tell me you jealous Lo? I told you, all you gotta do is give me the word, and I'll make it happen."

"No thank you, but, you have fun."

I said bye to Aaron, then walked to my studio so I could lock up and head home. I was just gone finish working from home, so I could walk around in my panties with my glass of wine. That is a perfect night for me.

THIRTY FOUR

Kiarra

When Lauren left, me and Kenzie took a nap, and I set an alarm so I could get up before Deontae made it home to start dinner. He told me earlier, he wanted fried chicken and spaghetti, and I took my chicken out to defrost.

My ringing phone ended my nap and hour early, and I woke up ready to snap on whoever it was calling.

"Hello?!"

"Don't answer the phone yelling and shit Kiarra, I will come over there and pop you in the mouth."

My bad ma, I was sleep when you called."

"What my grandbaby doing."

"She still sleeping, like I wish I was."

"Get over it, you're up now. I want to run something by you though."

"Wassup?"

"I want to move to Miami with Steph and Law, I'll still come back and you can visit."

"Dang you only been back for a year and you running away already?"

"It's nothing for me to do out here Chubbz. Imma miss not being down the street from you and my Kenzie boo, but I'm only a quick flight away."

"And what does Vince say about this?"

"His ass coming too, or he gon' be sitting right where he at."

I laughed at my mama and got out the bed to go start my dinner. "You are crazy. But, I guess I just gotta say ok and go with it."

"Thank you baby. I'm gone come get Kenzie tomorrow, she told me she missed me."

"Really ma, how did she tell you that?"

"She called me on the phone I got her, don't worry about all that."

"Ok, bye lady."

"Bye."

I put my phone on the counter, and cleaned my chicken before I seasoned them and put it in my flour.

When I was making my pasta Kenzie woke up, so I changed her diaper and put her in her high chair with a bottle.

Ding!

My text notification went off, and it was a message from Lo

This Nicki bitch want me to bless her face!

Oh gawd what happen now?

She sent me a screenshot of a post Nicki put up calling Lo a half ass photographer.

That bitch hating bestie, she mad cuz aint nobody buying that shedding ass dog hair she tryna sell!

Lmao! Right I'm glad I didn't get no hair from her. I had a damn leaf pile of weave left on the floor when them bitches left! Wyd tho?

Cooking…just had the best nap ever

I'm bout to go to sleep I'm irritated

Don't let that girl bother you.

It aint her… it's Adonis

Yo "friend" what did he do?

Nvm cuz you finna be real extra. Bye

Love you too!

I heard the front door open and close, before Deontae walked in and met me in the kitchen.

"It smells good in here."

"Thanks baby, how was work?"

"Same old, same old, saving lives, ya know."

"You so funny, go get cleaned up and the garlic bread should be done by then." He gave me a kiss and smack my butt before he kiss Kenzie on her cheek and went to the room.

Twenty minutes later, Deontae was walking out the room wearing basketball shorts, and no shirt. My eyes went right to his print and he laughed at me.

"You wild as hell bae, but if you tryna get something started put ZiZi in her play pen."

"Imma take you up on that offer after I eat."

I fixed his plate and I ate while breastfeeding Kenzie at the same time. She acted like she had to eat while everybody was eating, so this is what we did every night.

"What you do all day baby girl?"

"Nothing, caught up on my ratchet tv, and dealt with this little diva right here. I finally saw her trying to crawl."

"I told you she did it, you aint believe me."

We continued talking and eating, and Deontae helped me put the food up.

Kenzie played herself to sleep, so I laid her in her crib and turned the baby camera on.

When I walked into our bedroom, Tae had some music playing and he was laid across the bed with baby oil spread across his chest. I start laughing so hard I couldn't breathe.

"Baaaeee what the hell?"

"I'm tryna spice it up in here."

"You not gone do nothing but have one of us slide on the damn floor. It look like I'm about to throw you in the oven baby."

"Damn you going kinda hard on me baby."

"I'm sorry you look sexy as hell though." I took a towel and wiped some of the oil off his chest before I took my bottoms off straddled his lap.

"I love you so much Kiarra Blak."

"I love you too baby Mmmmm." I eased myself down on him and it was like he filled me up perfectly.

Rock on it like you a milly.

Bounce on it like you from Philly

So dope how you cut it up

Servin' a fiend I can't get enough

Tank's single *'F It UP'* was playing in the background, as I moved my hips to beat of the music. Tae was biting his lips and holding on to my waist so tight, I knew I was going to have his finger print on me by morning. The music went off and Deontae flipped me over so I was on my back and his sexy chocolate body hovered over me. He roughly kissed me and pinched my right nipple.

"Ooohhh bae it feels so gooooddd."

His face was twisted up as he moved in and out of me at quick pace causing my breast to bounce up and down with every stroke.

"Shit Ki! I'm finna cum baby, Aaarrgghh!" his body stiffened and I felt the goose bump on his arms. Deontae rolled off of me and I got up to get us a warm towel to clean up. I wiped him down and threw the towel in the dirty clothes hamper. Then I did the same to myself.

Deontae pulled me close to him and I wrapped one leg around him and went to sleep floating on cloud 9.

THIRTY FIVE

Church

Miranda ass had disappeared for a few days, and came back saying if I didn't marry her she was moving away with the kids, so I did it to shut her up. That little piece of paper made her feel like Queen Elizabeth or nothing.

Come to the blue house now!

Tre texted me, so I got up out the bed and start getting redressed.

"Where are you going Marshall?"

"I gotta handle some shit, I'll be back."

"Can we talk before you go?"

"Didn't I tell you I had some business to take care of? Why the fuck would you think I got time to sit and fucking talk?"

"I. Am. Your. Wife! You will not talk to me like I'm just some random hoe."

"Every time I get ready to leave, yo ass start with some damn bullshit. You always screaming you my fucking wife like I won't divorce yo ass. you supposed to be my peace, not adding to the fuck shit I gotta deal with!"

"Happy wife, happy life! I'm not happy so you need to satisfy me first."

"What the fuck you want now?"

"I want to have another baby."

"You on some bullshit, bye man I'll be back."

She rolled her eyes and threw herself back against the headboard. This girl was gone be reason I lost the little bit of patience I had left.

I rolled down 87th and parked behind our warehouse. I walked inside and Flip was hanging from the ceiling by a thick coil chain.

"Fuck going on in here?"

"Lil' nigga been stealing, tryna branch out and shit, with OUR SHIT. You really thought you was gon' get away with that shit?

"Naw man, I-I— I wasn't tryna steal, I was gone put the money back." Flip was whimpering like a little bitch.

Pow!

"Aaaahhhhh!!" Tre shot him in the knee and he was screaming like a little ass girl. I'm just glad this bitch was sound proof.

"Who else was in on the shit with you?"

"Nobody man, it was just me."

"You gone keep lying? Aite." I grabbed a seat and watched to see what Tre's ass was gone do next.

When he pulled a blow torch out I had to look at him like he was crazy.

"Wh-what you finna do with that man? Come on man please don't this, please— aahhh!!" Tre stood brought the torch to his bare chest and held it there, until Flip pissed on himself. It smell like barbecued nigga in here and I almost threw up.

"Aite man, just kill the nigga he aint talking."

"No! please, I'll talk, I'll tell you where they at."

"Who was it?"

"Maine, and boogie, they moving out of a house on 47th and Damen."

"Aite, bring him down Tre." Flip was lowered to the ground and I sent a shot through the middle of his head.

"Damn! You could've waited until I stepped back, got this punk nigga's blood all over my all white G fazos."

"Shut up and have somebody clean this shit up, you wanna play mad scientist and shit and I'm tired as hell."

I had been getting back on track with the organization, and trying to keep my mind off of Kiarra. It was hard, because she posted shit more and more, and it just made me miss her. I drove home smoking a blunt I rolled before I left, and all I could think about was all of the good memories we had.

Kiarra is stubborn, so I know I needed a miracle to get her to talk to me without pointing a gun in my face. I know how what I could to help me with her... and I don't play fair.

Epilogue

Lauren

Business has been booming as usual, and I had a few big names reaching out to work with me, I don't wanna say nothing yet to jinx it, but, know big things are coming my way.

Being single has to be one of the best decisions I ever made in my life. I do miss having somebody to drive me around, or bring me food, but that's what *Uber* and *Uber Eats* is for. The "men" of this generation can't handle me, my soul mate is either on his death bed, or not even born yet. I know one thing for certain; I got nothing but a wet ass and a headache when I fell in love with a dope boy, so my advice to you women.... Ruunnnnnn Biiihhhh!!

Adonis and I were still cool even though he tried to make me jealous with one of his little skeezers, and it worked for a little bit. But, the second I told him we couldn't kick it like that now that he had a girlfriend, he dumped her ass and was right back to tryna get me to go out with him on a "real date", I don't get why he insists on trying to mess up a good thing... we were good being friends with no benefits, no matter how much I wanted more. After Tre and Gio played me, I wasn't interested in pursuing nothing right not.

Speaking of Banks, I guess him and trout mouth is still doing whatever it is their doing, and that's all fine and dandy with me, but why this bitch gotta stalk me. Her smart/dumbass, must've been lurking because she liked one of my pictures. Like damn I dun gave you that nigga back, and I aint thinking about his ass, so why am I still being stalked? I aint got shit else to give her, except the number for a specialist to take care of the loose ass eye.

That's it for me though(maybe)... love, peace, and hair grease.

*****

Kodi

Things with me is going good, waaayy better from where I was before. I had been getting so many emails for deals, and people wanting to work with me, and I was super geeked. I wasn't ready to sign just yet, I'm kinda liking this independent artist stuff. Besides, I heard tooooo many crazy stories about record labels, and I did not want that kind of stress in my life right now.

Me and Gerald's relationship is blossoming beautifully and we had been thinking about moving in together. He had been pushing me so hard with my music, and I swear I really appreciate him. Even with all of the working we both do, he still makes sure that we go out and having our time alone. I can honestly say that I'm falling in love with him.

I'm still not fucking with my mom's side of the family, except for Koryn SOMETIMES. You gotta take her in doses, because she can work your nerves. But she was the only one who reached out to me on the daily. My other sister Krista, texted me once trying to get free tickets to a show I was headlining, and I had to block her ass. she was only reaching out because she wanted something. If she would've at least pretended to care about me I would've did it.

I reached out to my dad and he's supposed to make some arrangements for us soon. We'll see how that goes. Pray for me!

*****

Deontae

Kiarra texted me mad earlier because she just found out she was pregnant, but I was happy as hell. Kenzie was only 6 months and she kept saying how we were going to be spending all our money on diapers. She was acting like she was so upset, but I know she was just as excited as I was to add another little person to our family.

"What are you smiling so hard for Blak? I see every tooth in your mouth man."

"Kiarra just found out that she's pregnant again."

"Damn, y'all wasn't playing, was you? Having them back to back, aint least they'll be close in age. Are y'all done?"

"Hell naw, when she said those I do's, it was over from there, I'm tryna have a football team full."

Dr. Pierce whistled and patted me on my shoulder. "You're going to need a raise, and a second job brother. Congratulations though, you seem really happy... make me want to go find a Mrs. and settle down or something."

"Thank you, man, I'm about to get out of here, so I

can get some rest, I'll see you in the morning."

"Alright, I'm heading out right behind you, don't speed too hard to go make baby number 3."

"Baby number 2 didn't even come out yet."

"Shit the way y'all having 'em, she'll get double pregnant."

I laughed and dapped him before I walked out the door. I got on the elevator and texted Ki as I was walking to my truck.

Me: *I'm on my way home bae, I'm starving*

Kiarra: *Ok, I cooked meat loaf so you don't have to get anything*

Me: *Ok love you Mrs. Blak*

Kiarra: *Love you too baby*

"That must be Kiarra the way you're smiling." I jumped hearing the unexpected voice, and he quickly wrapped his arm around my neck. My seatbelt was on, so it wasn't much that I could do but try to fight him off.

"Aaarrgghh!!"

He shoved something sharp in my chest and all of the air left my lungs. He twisted it and blood started squirting all over my steering wheel from the wound. My breathing labored and I tried to stay as still as I could so I won't move the knife that was in me.

"I told her you'll never have her. And I told you, I meant what I said to her." He opened the back door and got out the car and left me bleeding all over my front seat. I tried to grab my phone but it was on the floor, and I was trying not to move that much. I saw the elevator doors open and Dr. Pierce stepped off. I laid on the horn until he looked my way.

BEEEEEEEEPPPPPPPPPPPPPPPPP   BEEP!   BEEP! BEEP!

I was laying on the horn and trying to get his attention. He finally looked my way and smiled.

"Damn, Blak, I thought you would've been gone by now. What's going on? OH SHIT! I NEED HELP OUT HERE!" He opened my door and checked my wound, then he grabbed his phone and called inside so he could get assistance.

"I need help in the Employee parking garage, we got Dr. Blak outside with a stab wound in his chest. Hurry and get as many hands as you can! Hold on Blak, they're coming. What the hell happened man? Who did this to you?"

"Ch-Church. Call Ki-Kiarra. Call. My. Wife. For. Me." It was hard for me to get my words out, but I wanted to make sure someone called Kiarra so she can get here. I needed to see her and my baby if this was going to be it for me.

"I got you, I got you. Don't try to talk, relax, they're coming, hold on for me Blak. Fuck! Fuck! Hurry up! His pulse is faint."

I was pulled out the front seat and rushed into the operating room. There was a bunch of noise, as I saw all the bright lights shining in my face. The medicine they gave me was taking over and I closed my eyes.

My thoughts drifted to my daughter, and I couldn't remember if I kissed her before I left out the house or not. I knew I wasn't making it out of this and it pissed me off because I wouldn't get to see my daughter grow up, or walk her down the aisle. I know my wife needs me as much as my kids do, but I know she's strong and going to hold down the home front. I told Kiarra I had her forever, and that's what I meant. Even in death.

******

Kiarra

I was getting my meatloaf out of the oven when I heard Kenzie scream like somebody was pinching her.

"What's the matter mommy baby, you ready to get out that stupid bouncer?" I picked her up and she stopped crying and start looking around the condo.

"You looking for daddy? He's on his way home, let's get your booty cleaned before he get here though." I changed her diaper and we sat watching tv and waiting for Deontae to get home. My cell phone rang and I thought it was Deontae calling me, because he should've been here by now. It wasn't Deontae, but Kim calling me, I started not to answer because I aint feel like hearing nobody's drama tonight.

"Hello?" There was a bunch a moving around before she came back on the phone

"Ki, you need to get down here now!" She was crying hysterically and I was starting to panic.

"What's wrong Kim, are you ok, what happened?"

"It's Deontae! Somebody stabbed him in the parking garage, hurry! He was bleeding so much and they told me to call you."

I hung up and I stood up to go get dressed. My head was spinning and I felt like I was going to pass out. I laid on the floor and called Lauren.

"Hey boo. Hello? Ki, what's wrong?"

"S-Somebody stabbed Deontae, I can't breathe Lo, I can't breathe please come help me."

"Ohmigod. I'm on my way bestie, stay on the phone."

I sat on the phone for twenty minutes crying and hyperventilating, while Lo was on the phone trying to calm me down. Lauren came in and got Kenzie dressed for me, while I tried to get myself together. I threw on some sweat pants and a hoodie, and threw a bunch of wipes and diapers in my purse. While I walked back out to the living room, Lo was standing by the door with Kenzie's car seat.

"It's gon' be ok boo, just think positive."

We rode to the hospital, and I felt like I was in a really bad dream that I couldn't wake up from. The closer we got to the hospital, the more my stomach started to hurt.

"Where's Deontae is he ok?" I ran to the nurse desk and I know I looked crazy with my red eyes and hair all over my head, but I needed answers.

"I-I'll go get someone just wait right here."

I saw Dr. Pierce and he looked like he was crying. I ran towards him and he tried to fix himself.

"Dr. Pierce! Where is he, is he ok?"

He didn't say anything, but he grabbed me and

hugged me tight. Even though he didn't say anything, it still said so much and I felt my heart instantly break.

"Noooo, please don't tell me he's gone, where is he? Let me go see, don't just give up on him, pleeeaasseeee. Go back in there Pierce!"

"He died on the table, the knife hit a major artery and he bled out. We tried everything, I'm so sorry Kiarra." He had tears running down his face, and he walked off.

I broke down in the middle of the floor and cried my little heart out not caring who was around and looking at me. What I supposed to tell our kids, Kenzie's too young, she won't remember him, and the new baby isn't even here yet. We haven't even been married for a year yet, and I'm a widow already.

"Ki, you have to get up, come on baby." Lo got on the floor with me and hugged me tight.

"Where's my baby?"

"Kim have her in the family room, let's get up so we can call his parents." I broke down crying again, because I had to break Mama Roxy, and Dave's heart, just like mine was.

"Kiarra wait." Dr. Pierce stopped me from walking and pulled me to the side.

"He said something when I found him, before he told me to call you."

"What did he say?

"Church. He just kept saying church. Do you know what that means?"

"No.... I don't, thank you Dr. Pierce."

I stomped to the family room, and Lo was standing by the door waiting on me.

"I called Gio, he's on the way. What's wrong Ki?"

"Church did this, I'm going to fucking kill him myself bestie."

"I got yo back baby, just let me know. But we gotta handle this right now."

I nodded in agreement and went in the room to hug my baby girl. I never wanted my kids to experience the pain of losing their father young like I did.

I heard some commotion and Banks came rushing in the room we were waiting in. "What happened? Kenzie ok?"

"Yes, she's ok...but...something else happened."

"Something like what, where Tae at?"

I stood frozen trying to find the best way to put this. There wasn't a good way to put this at all.... But here it goes.

*****

Banks

I don't know what the hell was going, I just got a text from Lauren saying get to the hospital now with Kiarra. but, now I'm standing here in front of Kiarra, and her eyes were blood shot red and her hair was all over the place.

"He's gone Banks. My husband is gone, he killed him." Kiarra broke down crying and I caught her before she hit the floor. She was crying in my chest and trying to talk but I couldn't make out nothing she was saying.

"You not making sense right now sis, who the fuck got killed I know you not talking about my bro?"

Kiarra looked me in my eyes, and said, "Church killed Deontae."

I stood staring at Kiarra waiting for her to say she was just playing or something, anything except that my cousin, and best friend was taken away from me. But, from the look in her eyes I knew she was serious.

"Fuuuuccckkkkk!!!" I walked away and punched the wall repeatedly until I couldn't feel the pain in it any-more.

"Gio, calm down, you fucking your hand up." Lau-ren grabbed me and I turned to her and laid my head on her shoulder. I know she didn't give a fuck about me anymore, but she let me cry like a newborn baby on her shoulder anyway.

"It's ok, you gotta stay strong, Kiarra is going to be a mess, and so is his parents. You gotta be strong and hold this family together." She was rubbing my back and talking lowly into my ear and I just stayed quiet and em-braced the moment.

"Gio? What's going? Why you crying you baby?"

Aunt Roxy and Uncle Dave walked in and I felt like shit for what I was about to tell them. Kiarra was crying too hard, so I knew she couldn't do it. I wiped my eyes, and walked to them.

"I'm sorry Tt." I got choked up and she they were both just standing there waiting for me to finish.

"Tae gone, he got killed Unc." Aunt Roxy grabbed her chest and fell back against Uncle Dave, who was trying to hold his own self up.

"What do you mean Giovanni? Where is my baby? Take me to my baby! Who did this to him? Father God whyyyyy?!?" She was crying and Uncle Dave had to lead her to a seat so she wouldn't fall out.

"You know who did this Gio?"

"I'm so sorry y'all, it was my ex this is all my fault."

"It's not your fault Kiarra, you can't control other people's actions. Don't start beating yourself up." Uncle Dave was trying to console Kiarra and his wife, and I was trying to keep my tears in. Kenzie started whining, so Kiarra wiped her face quickly and grabbed her from the white nurse I never even noticed before.

"I'll go see if he's ready to be seen yet, and I'll be back."

We all sat back waiting until she came back and led us to the room Deontae's body was. Everyone in the room was speechless. Kenzie was reaching for Tae and crying because Kiarra wouldn't put her down.

Looking at my cousin's body laying here lifeless, broke my fucking heart. He was all I had left besides my aunt and uncle. I know shit will never be the same, but I'm gone make sure I'm there for little Kenzie and Kiarra.

I walked out the room and Kiarra pulled me to the side. "Don't do nothing without me Banks." I smacked my lips and was about to walk about until she grabbed my arm again. "I'm not playing, he took my kids father away from them, and my husband away from me. I want to be the one to end his life."

She had that killer look in her eye, so I agreed and walked out the hospital. Church was going to feel me soon. I spared his life before but I'm not doing it again. His time was ticking.

To be continued...

More great reads from A. Jova'n :

Yedda &Swift: A Deranged Love Story 1&2

*The Risks We Take For Love & Money
1 (collab w/DeeAnn)*

*Caught Up With A Chi-Town Hitta:
A Forbidden Love 1&2*

Pretty Girls Get Down With Hood Niggas 1&2